NOW COMES THE SPRING

WARM DESIRE

His hazel eyes carried a sensual message that was impossible to ignore. They looked deep into hers, trying to judge her emotions and response. Tracy gazed back at him confidently; the feelings that he aroused were too primitive and too strong to pretend coyness. A delicious shiver of anticipation raced through her.

Could it be that he felt that same magnetic attraction that she kept experiencing? That same tingling excitement whenever they were together? It caused her blood to race as she imagined quite vividly the touch of his hands on her body.

Some of Tracy's desires must have glimmered in her eyes, for Josh did not move away from her after he closed her door. He gazed deep into her eyes for a long moment, drinking in the passion that was awakening there. Then slowly, he bent his head so that his lips touched hers in the gentlest of caresses. It was a whisper, a teasing touch . . .

Now Comes The Spring

Andrea Edwards

AVON
PUBLISHERS OF BARD, CAMELOT, DISCUS AND FLARE BOOKS

NOW COMES THE SPRING is an original publication of Avon Books. This work has never before appeared in book form.

AVON BOOKS
A division of
The Hearst Corporation
959 Eighth Avenue
New York, New York 10019

First Avon Printing, May, 1983

AVON TRADEMARK REG. U.S. PAT. OFF. AND IN OTHER COUNTRIES, MARCA REGISTRADA, HECHO EN U.S.A.

Printed in the U.S.A.

WFH 10 9 8 7 6 5 4 3 2 1

Chapter One

"I DIDN'T ASK for this assignment, you know," Tracy Monroe called out sharply, pulling on her navy, down-filled jacket. She hurried down the hallway after a rapidly moving pair of broad shoulders.

The shoulders stopped in front of the elevator and turned toward her. She was confronted with an icy glare. "Are you coming or not?" He did not pause for her answer, but marched into the elevator that had miraculously appeared.

"Damn!" Tracy muttered. Even the elevators obeyed him immediately. "Sorry!" She smiled an apology as the large black leather case she carried over her shoulder bumped into a young man getting off the elevator. He turned to smile back, clearly taken by her large blue eyes and generous mouth, but suddenly he was gone as the doors slid solidly shut. Tracy sighed slightly and shifted her camera case so she could zip up her jacket.

"What's the matter? Want to go back so you can give him your number?" Josh jeered, glancing down at her.

Tracy glared right back at him. "No," she snapped. "I was hoping I have all the lenses I need, since you couldn't give me time to check my bag."

His hazel eyes looked skeptical as he turned to face the doors, but Tracy tried to ignore her irritation with him, taking a white knitted cap out of one pocket and pulling it over her short dark brown curls. Josh Rettinger might be a good reporter, but he was an egotistical, arrogant, heartless son-of-a—

The elevator stopped and Tracy found herself running after Josh again, across the beige marbled floor of the lobby of Chicago's Tribune Tower and past the uniformed guard at his desk in front of the newspaper's Christmas tree. With dismay, she realized that Josh was getting farther and farther ahead of her. Why was it that everyone just naturally parted to let him by and closed ranks to impede her progress?

She supposed it could have something to do with the fact that he was about six feet tall, while she was barely five feet three inches. And his ruthless, cold stare did tend to intimidate people much more than her openly friendly gaze.

However brilliant the reasons for her slow progress, she doubted that they would go very far with him, and she renewed her efforts to catch up. She pushed through a group of schoolchildren who had come for a tour of the newspaper, and out the revolving doors. The frigid air swept along Michigan Avenue as in a wind tunnel, chilling her to the bone in spite of the large heaters that hung above the entrance to the building. She took a quick glance ahead of her to locate Josh's sheepskin jacket and then bent her head down to escape the force of the wind. She promptly charged right into Josh.

"What are you doing here now?" he barked.

Tracy looked up, ready to apologize, only to

find that she was still facing his back. She peered around his side to see an elegantly attired blonde standing before him, dressed in a calf-length suede coat in deep brown and a fur hat that must have cost as much as Tracy's beloved Nikon camera.

"We have to talk, Josh," the blonde informed him, not cowering from his obvious displeasure.

"Denise, this isn't the time," he told her, his voice softening slightly with regret.

Even if *he* was not aware of the people moving around them, Tracy was: she was jostled from behind as people tried to use the door she had just come out of. Shifting her case on her shoulder, she stepped to Josh's right, expecting him to move also, but the blonde had one hand on his left arm.

"You never have time," she complained. "There's always some damn story that's more important." The ice in her voice matched what was usually in his.

"It's my job, you know," he reminded her impatiently.

"And I'm supposed to be your fiancée." Her eyes got colder, if that was possible. "And I did not appreciate the message you left on my answering machine telling me we were going to your parents' home for Christmas. I have other plans that do not include Harvard, Illinois."

Tracy saw Josh's lips tighten, and she glanced uneasily around her, wishing she could somehow disappear. Much as she disliked Josh, she had no desire to be a witness to a rather personal quarrel; but it was hard to appear interested in the Tribune Tower or the Wrigley Building across the street. What idiot would be standing in the windiest spot in the city, admiring the local architecture, when the windchill was twenty-two below zero?

"Look, Denise, my father just got out of the hospital and my whole family is going up for the holiday," Josh explained with little patience. "It seemed like the ideal time for you to meet them, and it's not as if you have any family around here you were going to see."

"No family?" Denise cried. "Andrea Redmon means more to me than any family! You know how long I've worked to get an invitation to her Christmas party. Think of the influential people I'll meet and what it'll do for my career! I can meet your family anytime, but Andrea's party is a once-in-a-lifetime chance for me."

At such an uncaring remark, Tracy gave up all pretense of being polite and uninterested and turned to watch Josh. Apparently she was not the only curious bystander, for behind her, the steady rhythm of the Salvation Army bell-ringer had slowed considerably.

Unaware of his audience, Josh's face had paled under the wind-induced flush. "With my father's health as precarious as it is, I'm not certain that you *can* meet them anytime," he pointed out, his voice very quiet and deadly. "As for your precious singing career, I would think you'd be better off getting some experience at some of the smaller clubs in the city than hoping you'll meet someone at a party to give you your big break."

"You know nothing about the entertainment circles I move in," Denise sniffed haughtily. "And that party is vital to my career." She turned to walk away, but Josh's hand grabbed her.

"You'd better make a choice then," he informed her. "Because my fiancée is coming up to Harvard with me."

"That's no choice at all," she laughed loudly and pulled off first her glove, then a solitaire diamond ring. She dropped the ring into his outstretched hand. "You certainly weren't much fun anyway." She smiled knowingly to the people about who had caught her last remark.

A dull red flush crept over Josh's face as his fingers closed around the ring. He slipped it into his pocket and turned away, not bothering to watch Denise go. Unfortunately, Tracy did not move fast enough and he stepped on her.

"What the hell are you standing around here for?" he snapped, suddenly noticing her presence. "We've got to get moving if we're going to get those pictures I need."

"You've got to be kidding." Exasperated, Tracy eyed the windswept flat roof of an old apartment building that Josh had led her up to.

"Why would I be kidding?" He frowned at her briefly, then walked over to the edge to look down the three stories to the ground.

Why would he be kidding, indeed? Tracy thought to herself. He probably doesn't even know how to kid. "Have you noticed it's cold up here?" she asked as she joined him at the edge of the roof.

He glanced at her, then turned back to watch the scene below them. They were in a mixed residential and small-industrial area southwest of downtown Chicago. To their left were a number of small businesses, scattered among worn-looking apartment buildings and two-family houses. In the other direction lay an old red-brick high school.

Its classical style with high-arched doorways and Latin inscriptions contrasted sharply with its graffiti-covered outside walls.

"This is the perfect place to wait," Josh told her. "Nobody will notice us up here, and when he starts selling the drugs to the kids, we can get his picture."

"Yeah," Tracy agreed and looked around her. At least one advantage of the gale-force winds that swept the roof was that there was no snow left to melt through her jeans. She found a spot protected by a low wall and sat down, digging through her bag for her light meter and various lenses. In order to work better, she had had to remove her gloves; her fingers quickly went numb from the cold.

She had only six pictures left on her roll, and decided to use them up before their subject arrived. She took a picture or two of the roof, then pointed the camera at Josh. He was scowling at her.

"Try and look pleasant," she suggested. "If it kills you, I promise to call the paramedics."

She thought he would ignore her, but, for a minute, he dropped the cynical air and let a warmer expression cross his face. Tracy was surprised at how handsome he actually was and clicked away, finishing up her roll of film.

"Now, that wasn't so painful, was it?" she teased as she removed the leather protective case from around the camera. "What were you thinking of? A good meal? Someplace warm and cozy?"

His glare had returned and he favored her with it briefly before he turned back to watching the street below. "I was thinking of your smashed and battered body after I threw you off the roof."

"Oh." She changed the roll of film in silence, and sat back to wait.

"Why can't you investigate this cop in the summer?" she muttered after a few minutes of silent freezing.

Josh settled himself down along the wall that went around the edge of the roof. "What's this preoccupation with the cold? Where'd you grow up? In Florida?"

"No, in Elmhurst. A whole fifteen miles west of Chicago," she shot back, putting her hands under her arms to thaw them out.

"Then you should be used to the cold," he said, dismissing the subject.

Tracy watched him, wondering what he was feeling, if anything, about his broken engagement. He had not mentioned it in the car as they drove over here, but then he wasn't exactly the confiding type. Nor was he the sort that you could extend any sympathy to, even if he *was* attractive under his scowl. Good old Denise was probably lucky to be rid of him.

Instead of any personal conversation, he had briefly told her about his investigation of a policeman who had chased the drug dealers away from a high school, only to take over their business himself. Josh had wanted a photographer to catch him in the act of selling the drugs, but was clearly skeptical of Tracy's ability to do so.

After screwing on her telephoto lens, Tracy replaced her camera in her bag and settled back to wait. She huddled against the wall, not bothering to look down into the street. Even though Josh had shown her a picture of the man he was after, she was not likely to recognize him, and Josh would tell her when he arrived.

"When did he come the other days?" she asked, trying to burrow her head down into the neck of her jacket.

"During the kids' lunchtime and after school," Josh murmured absently.

Tracy did not bother to ask him anything else. Her stomach was telling her that it was well past lunchtime, so hopefully their prey would come before she froze to death. Even if he didn't, though, she would not complain. Josh already thought she was a nuisance, and she was going to show him that she was as good a photographer as any man.

She didn't know why she constantly felt she needed to prove herself, she thought crossly, although she had to admit that since she came to work for the *Tribune* two years before, she had felt that way less and less. There were only a few reporters, Josh being the worst of them, who preferred not to work with her.

She could understand some of their hesitations, especially on the sports desk. It was a lot easier to get the right picture if you understood the game, but there were times when no sports photographer was available and Tracy was called. She was getting better with baseball and soccer, but hockey still eluded her. Her pictures always seemed to miss the real action.

City Hall beat was another area where she lacked experience and the necessary contacts, but she could snap pictures at a press conference or wait around the exit from the city council room as well as anyone.

Most of her assignments, however, were covering breaking stories—fires, accidents, and the like—so she had been surprised when she was assigned to work with Josh on his investigative piece. She knew that his reaction to her presence would hardly be delight, but she decided not to switch assignments with another photographer. Josh was really the last remaining diehard, and every chance she had to work with him would help to erase his opposition to her.

Someday, she dreamed, he would ask for her specifically because she was so good. And since his stories often attracted national attention, her photographs would also become nationally known.

It might take a while to achieve that goal, but Tracy was patient. She had worked for a local weekly newspaper in the suburbs for four years before coming to the *Tribune*, and she had taken every assignment she could to build up her experience and her name. It had been hard to make people notice her when, week after week, she snapped pictures of gourmet meals and grand openings of new stores, but every so often a really good chance came her way. She had won awards from the Chicago Press Photographers Association five times and twice from the National Press Photographers Association. Now, at twenty-seven, she felt her career was really on its way.

"There's his car," Josh said suddenly, breaking into her thoughts.

Tracy rose stiffly to her knees and peered over the wall at the small dark green car pulled up to the sidewalk across the street. "Lousy angle," she noted. "You won't see anything but the car and the kid at the window. Hardly proof of drug dealing," she added.

"He'll get out of the car," Josh insisted as they watched, but the shadowy figure remained stubbornly inside.

"Why doesn't he get out?" he muttered while they watched several children walk casually up to the car and leave after a moment. "This isn't his pattern at all."

Tracy took a couple of pictures, even though she knew they wouldn't show much. "Maybe it's too cold," she suggested, sitting back on her heels and pulling her gloves on again.

Josh ignored her. "I wonder if it's the same guy." He peered down at the car.

"Why don't you go down and ask him?"

He turned to look at her but, rather than the hard stare she'd expected, he had a thoughtful gleam in his eye. "That's an idea," he said, his eyes traveling over her plain jacket and worn denim jeans. "Not me, of course. But you could."

"Hey, I'm not the reporter," she protested weakly. "I'm only here to take pictures."

"Be reasonable. I'm thirty-five," he said with a certain amount of reluctant charm. "With the gray in my hair, I can't even pass for a college student; but you don't look that different from a high school kid."

Although the way he said it was no compliment, Tracy knew it was true. Wasn't she always carded when she went into a bar? She glanced at Josh's tanned face, at the tiny wrinkles around his eyes and streaks of gray running through his dark hair; she knew he looked too experienced and sure of himself to go down past the car without attracting attention.

She put down her camera. "What would I have to do? Just walk past the car and look at him?"

His sudden smile did not fool Tracy. It was not because of any personal warmth toward her, but because he had gotten his way. "Maybe you could stop a minute and look nervous, like you've never bought drugs before."

Tracy looked at him warily. "You mean you actually want me to buy something from him?"

"Sure. That's the best way to see if he's really a dealer. Maybe you can even get him out of the car," he said hopefully, picking up her camera. "How do you work this thing?"

Reluctantly, Tracy pointed out the viewfinder. "It's already focused for the distance, so all you'll have to do is look through here and press the shutter." She showed him the button on the top of the camera. "And don't drop it," she added, but he was already looking through it and lining up his subject. "Hey, what am I supposed to use for money?"

He glanced up at her as if she was becoming more of an irritation, then pulled his wallet from his back pocket and handed her a twenty-dollar bill. "Now will you go down and see if he's the guy whose picture I showed you?" he snapped, his thin layer of charm showing a few bare spots. Tracy saluted his back in mockery, then walked over to the stairs.

How did he expect her to lure the guy out of the car? Tracy wondered as she went down the stairs and out onto the sidewalk before the building.

She crossed the street uneasily, resisting the temptation to glance up at Josh as she fingered the twenty in her pocket. Why had she let herself go along with his crazy scheme? This was certainly not going to convince him of her skill as a photographer, just that she was an insane woman who could be talked into anything.

Her anger carried her across the street and she suddenly found herself next to the plain, dark green car. Her feet stopped moving when she spotted the heavyset man inside. He was watching her as he absently fingered his mustache.

"Ya want somethin', honey?" he called to her quietly.

Tracy nodded as she took a step closer and pulled the money from her pocket.

He frowned when he saw the twenty. "That all?" he growled. "I ain't no dime store, you know." He turned away for a moment, then proffered a small package.

Tracy held out the money to him, but just before he caught hold of it, the wind whipped it from her fingers and blew it down the street.

Damn! she thought as she raced after it. Josh would be convinced that she was incompetent now.

It actually had only blown about thirty feet before she caught it. Turning around with it clutched tightly in her fingers, Tracy discovered that the man had gotten out of the car and followed her. Grimly he took the money from her hand while Tracy blinked, momentarily blinded by a glare of light.

The man noticed the glare also, and spun around in time to see Josh on the roof across the street. Light from the sun was reflecting off the camera lens and into their faces.

"Shit!" the man snarled and whirled around to

grab the bag back from Tracy. With the side of his arm, he swung at her viciously, knocking her off her feet. She fell to the sidewalk, landing sharply on her left hand. A flash of pain sped up her arm.

"Damn," she muttered, leaning on her right hand to get up. The man had not gone back to his car but was running across the street; he disappeared into Josh's building. "If anything happens to that camera, I'm going to kill him," Tracy promised herself and raced across the street.

It was dark inside the building after the bright sunlight outside, and Tracy had to climb the first flight of stairs slowly until her eyes grew accustomed to the dim light. By the time she had passed the first landing, and she could have gone faster, she began to go slower. What in the world was she doing, following a drug dealer into a dark and deserted stairway?

She could hear a loud voice coming from the roof. It wasn't Josh's, and she was picturing him lying dead or severely wounded. Her camera was, no doubt, destroyed along with him.

The sound of running footsteps coming toward Tracy awoke a sense of urgency in her, and she fled down the hallway of the second floor just as the drug dealer raced past her down the stairs. Once he was out of the building, Tracy crept up the last flight of stairs and out onto the roof.

Josh was nowhere in sight, but her camera case and all her lenses and film were scattered across the roof as if someone had kicked them in anger. She ran over to scoop the things up. Her wide-angle lens was scratched and her light meter was broken. That meant Josh probably still had her camera. It had better be in one piece, or he wouldn't be! she vowed. As she picked up the pieces and put them back into her case, she felt like crying.

Damn Josh! Where was he, anyway? she wondered as she looked around quickly. He must have gone part of the way down the stairs and hidden on one of the floors as she had.

Tracy looked over the wall in time to see the dark green car speed away, then she picked up her case and walked down the stairs. It was luck she remembered where Josh had parked the car, she thought as she came out of the building. A quick glance around showed no sign of the drug dealer's car, so she hurried down the block and around the corner, rehearsing the angry speech she was about to deliver to Josh.

When she rounded the last corner, her feet stopped in sudden confusion. The parking place was empty. Josh and the car were gone.

Tracy stared at the empty spot in bewilderment for a long moment, oblivious to the sounds of the traffic around her. What did he expect her to do? Take the bus back to the paper?

"Damn it, wake up, will you?"

Tracy looked up at the shout to see Josh and his car in the street before her. Several cars stopped behind him were beeping irritably. She ran quickly toward his car and jumped in just as he was pulling away.

"I thought you'd left," she explained with a laugh.

"I would have if I'd known you'd be standing about daydreaming," he growled.

Tracy ignored both the slight stiffness in her left

wrist and his rudeness as she picked up her camera, looking it over carefully.

"I didn't break it," he noted sarcastically.

"Well, my light meter and who knows what else *were* broken because you left them on the roof," she retorted, continuing her inspection of the camera.

He just shrugged. "The paper'll replace them. It was worth it for the pictures I got."

Tracy's anger subsided slightly. She put the camera down. "They were good?" she asked eagerly.

"I think so," he said, keeping his eyes on the road and not bothering to look at her. "Let's just hope you can blow them up decently."

Leaning back against the car seat with a defeated sigh, Tracy realized that she was back where she had started. All of her efforts to gain his approval had been for nothing. He still doubted her ability as a photographer.

Chapter Two

WHEN ONE GOT OFF the elevator on the fourth floor at the *Tribune*, it seemed like a quiet, subdued place to work, with its white walls and dark gray carpeting. A few steps down the hall, though, and reality set in, for muted colors and lights did not go with the fourth-largest daily newspaper in the country.

Around a corner, down a hallway, and the peaceful atmosphere was gone. The huge room housed the sports, financial, and features departments amid the tall white cabinets that surrounded each desk. The center of the room was the city room: the news department, home for both Josh and Tracy during most of the day.

The city room was huge, with white walls, although little actual wall space was visible. One wall was covered with venetian-blinded windows, while narrow black lockers took up some room near the picture desk. Most of the rest was hidden by the coffee machine, file cabinets, and shelves piled high with books and maps. Reporters' desks were crowded in everywhere, each with its own keyboard and monitor; some, at the far end of the room where the copy editors sat, had two monitors.

Next to the copy editors, along the windows, two offices for the editors were partitioned off.

Freestanding bookshelves and slightly larger desks could be seen in them through the glass walls, along with a few plants.

At the other end of the room, near the coffee machine and admittedly a much better location, the picture desk was located. It was there that Tracy and the other photographers were given their assignments, sometimes through the two-way radios that they carried or, if they were back at the newspaper, from Al himself—their boss.

Down the hall was the darkroom and the picture file. It was there that the street photographers developed the black-and-white prints they took and the color studio printed their layouts. Also in the photo lab was the machine that transferred the laser photos from UPI and AP.

Tracy could see Josh as she walked from the photo lab. His desk was in the middle of the room, but he had his back to the main aisle. At one time, she had heard, he had faced it, but had threatened to make obscene gestures to the tour groups that stopped there to see the city room. His desk was changed. Must be nice to have such power, she thought, feeling tired and hungry and looking forward to getting something to eat. She was not pleased to discover as she approached his desk that he was on the telephone.

"I know it's only three days until Christmas, Dan, but something's come up and I can't make it after all," he was saying into the phone.

Tracy caught his eye and put the photos on his desk, but he held up his hand for her to wait. Great, she thought, leaning her back against his desk and staring across the room at a silver Christmas tree on top of a file cabinet. She'd give him two minutes to finish his conversation and then she was leaving.

"I'll call Mother and tell her myself," Josh said impatiently. "I wasn't expecting you to tell her." As he listened, Josh slipped the photos out of the envelope she had put them in and frowned at them. He tossed them aside suddenly and leaned back in his chair. "I know, I know," he snarled. "Everyone's going to be there. I'm sure no one will miss me then. In fact, they'll probably be relieved I won't be there."

Well. Tracy's eyebrows raised thoughtfully. So Denise had won! Somehow she hadn't expected Josh to give in to Denise's demands, and she felt vaguely disappointed in him. She thought he had more guts than that.

"Yeah, Merry Christmas to you, too." Josh's voice hardly reflected the Christmas spirit as he slammed down the phone. "These pictures aren't any good," he announced and shoved them across the desk to her. Tracy turned around to face him.

"What do you mean they're no good?" she cried angrily. She picked them up and flipped through them herself. "I thought they came out great."

He grabbed one away from her and pointed to the man in the center. "But he's not the cop I'm investigating," he explained. "They must have gotten wind of the investigation and sent someone else."

"That's hardly my fault," she noted curtly. "We took what you wanted to take, and they came out fine."

"Yeah, they're great," he mocked her. "Maybe

you can make up a couple of dozen for me for my Christmas cards."

Tracy was furious. She had done her job and done it well, yet he was blaming her for the wrong man being in the pictures. "Just because you're mad that you caved in to Denise's demands is no reason to take it out on me," she said, trying to keep her voice from quivering with anger. She threw the pictures down on his desk and turned away.

"It's none of your damned business what I do," he informed her.

"Monroe!" someone bellowed across the room. Tracy looked over to see her boss waving to her. She had another assignment before she left for the day. As she went over to get the details, she saw Josh pick up his coat and storm out.

It was well past nine o'clock by the time Tracy returned to the newspaper. Once the pictures of the mayor and the head of the transit union shaking hands over a new contract were developed and approved, she didn't know what she was likely to die of first: exhaustion or starvation.

The brisk night air woke her up when she left the building, and she decided to walk to Billy Goat's Tavern for something to eat before she drove home. Located on lower Michigan Avenue, it was a favorite gathering place for everyone at the newspaper, from pressmen to editors, although it was anything but warm and friendly. The grillmen felt it was their duty to insult everyone who came in, and, in case they missed a few, there were enough posters covering the walls to fit any occasion—from a picture of pressmen sitting on bar stools with dirty pants to a "Thanks for Leaving" sign. The place was bright, noisy, and relaxing.

The tavern was crowded, as it always was, though at this time of night there were more drinkers than eaters. Tracy was the only one at the grill in the center of the room, a fact that didn't stop the grillman from yelling at her to hurry up with her order and to keep the line moving. When a place had a reputation for insults, she supposed they had to keep practicing.

Once her "doobla cheeseborger" was cooked and wrapped in waxed paper, she paid for it and a bag of potato chips, then looked around for a place to sit. The hustling young black waiter took her bar order and handed her a foaming stein of beer. Since there were no such niceties as trays, and she did not trust her balancing act, her search for a seat grew a little more desperate. There were a few inebriated offers that she ignored as she skirted the "Nanny" and "Billy" signs above the hallway to the bathrooms and peered into the VIP Room. She spotted Josh back in one corner. If he didn't mind sharing a corner of his table, she could at least eat in peace.

"Do you mind if I sit here?" she asked him. "There aren't any empty tables."

He looked up at her with a frown. "If you expect to see me crying my heart out into my beer, you'll be disappointed."

"I don't expect to look at anything but some dinner," she muttered and sat down facing the mural of the tavern's original owner and his pet billy goat. They looked relatively harmless painted up on the wall, but as every loyal Cubs fan knew, they were more dangerous than the Dodgers.

Apparently the old man had liked to have his pet with him at all times, or else the animal had had a fondness for baseball. Whatever the reason, when he had taken the goat to Wrigley Field to watch a Cubs baseball game, and the goat was refused admittance, the man had placed a curse on the Cubs. And a mighty strong curse it had been, for even when Wrigley Field management backed down in 1982 and allowed the goat to enter the park, the Cubs still continued to lose. Of course, since the original goat was long since dead, perhaps it was not possible to rectify the slight through one of its descendants. The Cubs might be doomed to lose forever, Tracy thought absently, but at least they had a good reason. Better than the Sox, or the Bears or the Bulls . . . She stopped, suddenly conscious of Josh's eyes on her.

"I did not give in to Denise's demands," he said abruptly. "I don't know why you thought I had."

She took a long drink of her beer. "Well, I heard you say you weren't going up to your parents' for Christmas, so I assumed you were staying here with Denise," she explained as she took a bite of the kaiser-roll-encased hamburger.

"As a liberated career woman yourself, I take it you think I should back down?" His voice was quiet, but Tracy was not fooled. She could hear the anger lying underneath.

"Since I don't know either you or Denise, I'm hardly qualified to tell you what to do," she pointed out coldly and ripped open her bag of potato chips. Sensing his exasperation with her evasiveness, she went on before he had a chance to speak. "From the little I heard, though, I thought that a visit to Harvard, Illinois, would not be ranked as a high point in her life.''

He smiled and drank down the last of his beer. ''You've been to Harvard, I take it?''

''I took pictures at the annual milk festival a couple of years ago,'' she told him, then added with a grin, ''Any town that can dream up a reason to get people to watch a girl take a bath in milk can't be too dull.''

He smiled slightly and waved at the waiter for another beer. ''I'm not staying here because I want to be with Denise,'' he told her abruptly after the man brought it over and Josh gave him a single. ''I just can't go up there without her.''

Tracy wondered how many beers he had had before she arrived. She doubted that this sudden verbosity was caused by her delightful personality. ''You may change your mind tomorrow,'' she said lightly, finishing her potato chips. ''Surely your family would understand that engagements get broken.''

''Yeah,'' he admitted gruffly. ''But my family's not the problem. It's me.''

Tracy said nothing. She was starting to feel sorry for him, and that was the signal for her to leave before it was too late. The long list of rescued dogs and cats that had passed through her life could attest to her soft heart. She took a long drink of her beer.

''You see, Monica will be there and I can't face her alone.''

Tracy put down the stein, a curious expression on her face. ''Who's Monica?''

Josh looked over at her, his eyes blinking rapidly as if he was having trouble focusing them.

"She's my ex-wife," he admitted with an embarrassed shrug.

"Why would she be there?" Tracy asked. Her resolve for a quick exit vanished. "Is she close to your family?"

His lips tightened briefly as he forced a smile onto his face. "You might say that. You see, she's married to my cousin now."

"Oh."

Tracy stared at him, seeing him for the first time as a person, not just an extremely demanding reporter. She realized with a shock that there was something about him that she found attractive. It wasn't just his hazel eyes that were framed by long, thick lashes, or his dark-brown hair that was streaked with gray. There was a vitality in his manner that commanded respect, and seemed to draw Tracy like a magnet, attracting her to him against her will. Some instinct of self-preservation made her look away, and she concentrated on what was left of her dinner.

Josh did not seem to notice her withdrawal. He picked up his bottle and drank the beer slowly. "I suppose you think I'm a coward not to want to face Monica alone," he said.

"No, I can understand it," she admitted, her mouth full of cheeseburger. It would be hard to face David in that situation, she knew. "But I think you might regret letting her keep you away."

He stared down at the wet rings his bottles had made on the red-checked Formica tabletop, absently moving his present bottle around, disrupting the designs. "It's not just her. Everyone's uneasy when I'm around. When I told them I was engaged they were all delighted. To them, it meant

30

that I was finally over Monica." He looked up at her. "It's all so stupid!" he sighed. "I'd just like to spend a quiet Christmas with my family, yet if I don't show up with Denise on my arm, no one else will enjoy the holiday." He looked at the bottle in his hand with sudden distaste, then pushed it away. "God, this stuff tastes terrible," he said and, folding his arms across the table, he laid his head down on them.

"Josh, you can't go to sleep here," Tracy cried, and shook his arm. He picked up his head and glared at her.

"Why not? It'll make a good bit of gossip for you to spread at the paper tomorrow," he snapped.

Tracy, suddenly used to his surliness, ignored his words. She got to her feet and walked around the table to his side. "Come on, Josh, some fresh air will do you good."

He muttered something she chose to ignore, but rose to his feet reluctantly. She led him through the tavern, up the few steps to the door, and outside.

Lower Michigan Avenue was tightly enclosed by buildings on either side and upper Michigan Avenue overhead. The air was stuffy and smelled of automobile exhaust, for the few side streets that led down to it did not provide much circulation. It wasn't until Josh and Tracy had walked up the steep incline on Hubbard to the regular street level that Josh actually got some fresh air. He did not immediately wake up, though, but continued his morose shuffle.

"Lord, but it's cold tonight," Tracy said with a shiver, expecting, or rather hoping, for some response from him. There was none. They walked another block in silence.

"I think you ought to let me drive you home," she told him. He still said nothing and she was not sure, as they walked to her car, whether he had even heard her, although it seemed highly unlikely that he was just walking this way with her because his car was parked right next to hers. When she stopped at her little blue Chevette, he stopped too.

"You know what I need?" he asked her suddenly, leaning against the car next to hers.

"A cup of black coffee?" she suggested. She unlocked her car and let him climb in, wondering how he was ever going to fit his long body into the tiny space. But he didn't seem to notice that his knees were up under his chin. She walked around to her side with a sigh and got in.

"I need a fiancée," he said quite matter-of-factly as she fastened her seat belt and started the engine.

"Right," she laughed and backed the car out of the space. "Maybe you can rent one." After paying for her parking, she turned to him. "Where do you live?"

Josh was leaning his head back against the seat, and looked about ready to fall asleep. "Hyde Park," he murmured.

"Hyde Park?" she repeated in dismay. In the opposite direction from her Uptown apartment, it would add another hour's driving before she would get home, and it was already 10:30! She pulled the car out into the street. Well, what difference did one more stray animal make? "If you promise to behave I'll let you have my sofa for the night," she informed him.

"No need to worry," he yawned. "I'm no threat to anyone. Just ask Monica," he added bitterly, and fell asleep.

"There. Now you guys won't be able to knock this down," Tracy told two midnight black kittens the next evening. They were sitting side by side on the back of her brown plaid sofa, watching her tie a string from her Christmas tree to a small hook she had anchored in the wall.

They did not look impressed when she knelt down to reach under one end table and a wooden rocker to pick up the painted wooden ornaments they had knocked down. Their eyes did flicker with interest, though, as she began hanging the ornaments back up, moving around the tree that filled up her bay window so nicely.

Tracy loved her old apartment. At the northern edge of Uptown, it was not exactly a popular neighborhood. The buildings were old, some in great need of repair, and the residents were mixed racially and economically. Still, the crime rate for her area was not as bad as the Uptown statistics seemed to indicate, and she didn't know of any other place in the city where you could get such large apartments for so little rent.

She lived on the second floor of an old building of "railroad flats," so named because the rooms were laid out in a narrow line, like a train. Her living room and her front door were in the front of the building and her kitchen was in the rear, with her back door opening onto a small wooden porch that served as a landing for the outside stairway and housed her garbage can. In between were the bathroom, bedroom, and a small dining room. Unfortunately, only the two end rooms had windows, and the heating was somewhat erratic in the winter; but those small disadvantages, Tracy thought as she finished hanging the rest of the ornaments, were outweighed considerably by the fact that pets were allowed.

"Now you two find something else to do besides destroy the apartment," she scolded the cats as she climbed down off the end table that she had used as a step stool. She brushed her hands off on the snugly fitting jeans that certainly did justice to her trim figure. While she was tucking her red ruffled blouse back into her pants, a buzzer rang on her stove to tell her that her dinner was done. Tracy hurried down the hall and into the kitchen.

A wheat-colored Irish terrier was sleeping on the beige tile in front of the oven. He opened one eye when Tracy leaned over him and took the chicken-and-rice dish out of the oven. She carried it over to the small round table in the corner, but before she could sit down to enjoy her meal, the doorbell rang.

"Shush, Paddy," she told the dog. He was growling quietly, although he didn't move when Tracy hurried back to the living room, noticing with a sigh that two ornaments were on the floor again. Standing on tiptoe, she peered through the tiny peephole in her door. Josh was standing there, looking rather uneasy.

Trying to hide her surprise, she pulled open the door. "Hi," she said and stepped aside to let him in. She had not seen him at all that day. The couch had been deserted when she got up that morning and she had been out of the city room on assignments all day. "Recovered from your hangover?

Or are you one of those fortunate people who never get them?''

His smile did not quite reach his eyes. ''Oh, I got one all right,'' he admitted and glanced around the room. ''Did I come at a bad time? You weren't going out or anything?''

''Not me.'' She shook her head; her dark curls bounced delightfully around her face. ''It's too cold to go out if you don't have to.'' She took his coat and hung it up on the brass coatrack next to the door, forcing her eyes away from the faded jeans and white turtleneck sweater that emphasized his rugged handsomeness. She was not pleased to realize that her breath had quickened and that her cheeks were flushed because of his arrival. She turned away, forcing her voice to be light. ''I was about to eat. Want to join me?''

''Oh, no,'' he said quickly, following her as she walked off toward the kitchen. ''I just wanted to apologize for last night. I don't usually make such a fool of myself.''

Tracy took another white plastic plate out of a cabinet and some silverware from a drawer. ''I'm having a glass of wine, but I can also make you some coffee, or I might even have a beer,'' she offered as she pulled the table from the wall so there would be room for them both to sit.

''Wine would be fine,'' he shrugged, watching her move around the warm, cozy kitchen. The cool dark brown and white furnishings seemed to highlight her warmth and sparkle. ''I really didn't mean to barge in like this.''

The dog got up slowly and went over to sniff Josh's feet, his tail wagging furiously. There was a loud crash from the living room, followed by two black streaks scurrying into the kitchen, where they jumped into a carpeted cat house in one corner.

"What was that?" Josh asked, surprised that Tracy continued to pour his wine as if nothing had happened.

"I imagine the Christmas tree fell down again," she laughed. "It's not quite steady enough for climbing. Come and sit down."

Josh walked over to the table, eyeing the cat house, where a scuffle seemed to be taking place. "You have a lot of creatures around here," he noted with the first genuine smile Tracy had seen on his face.

"Those two will be going soon." She nodded toward the kittens, ignoring the melting effect his smile had had on her stomach. "I'm only keeping them until Tree House gets rid of a few more of their older kittens."

"Tree House?" he asked as she pushed the casserole over to his plate.

"It's an animal shelter a block north on Carmine. I take care of extra or sick animals for them. Paddy," she nodded toward the dog, "is a diabetic and needs insulin shots each morning and a strict diet. The shelter isn't the best place for him to stay. He almost got a permanent home last week, but it fell through. But he's such a sweetheart of a dog, I'm sure somebody'll want him soon."

"Sounds like you take in all the strays," he noted, buttering a thick slice of Italian bread. "Is that what I was last night?"

She laughed at his embarrassed look. "You were certainly the biggest thing I ever brought home with me. I'm sure my mother would have been shocked.''

"I was quite shocked myself when I woke up,'' he said stiffly. "It's not the sort of thing I do regularly.''

Tracy did not look concerned and began to eat. "I understood. You were upset about Denise.''

"Hardly,'' he admitted wryly. "She was not the love of my life. I was mad that she had upset my plans, that's all.''

Tracy took a drink of wine. "So, have you changed your mind now that you're sober?''

Josh pushed the plate away from him even though he had barely touched the food, and played with his wine glass, his eyes unable to meet hers. "I thought a lot about everything you said last night, and I decided you were right.''

"I was?'' Tracy asked, trying to remember just which words of wisdom she had been spouting, but couldn't. "Anything to help.'' She reached over and took a slice of bread for herself.

"At first I thought your suggestion to rent a fi- ancée was stupid,'' he said, not noticing Tracy's gulp of surprise. "But the more I thought about it, the more sense it made.''

"It did?'' she asked weakly, turning to stare at him.

He nodded seriously. "I just need someone to put my family at ease. To make them think I'm not secretly lusting after Monica. My father's not well, and this could be our last Christmas all together.''

"So, where did you find a fiancée to rent?''

"That's the problem,'' he sighed. After a quick glance up at her, he looked back down at his glass. "I don't know how to find somebody.'' He took a deep breath. "I was hoping you could do it for me," he added in a rush.

Tracy felt as if she had stopped breathing. "Pretend to be your fiancée?" she asked in a whisper.

He seemed to gain courage from the fact that she had not refused him outright. "I've thought it all out," he assured her. "I want to hire you for a job, so I'd be willing to pay. I have no idea just what kind of rates one charges for this sort of thing, but I was sure we could come to some sort of agreement."

"Why me?" she asked, even more stunned by his businesslike attitude than by his original announcement. "We don't even like one another very much."

Josh just shrugged. "I don't see what difference that makes," he said. "I need someone I can trust, that isn't going to spread this all around the newsroom. I fully expected to hear about Denise's departure or my drunken confessions today, yet I didn't hear anything."

"Why would I tell everyone that?" she asked, rather annoyed.

"You didn't. I realized that immediately," he said. "But a lot of people would have, so I know that I can trust you."

Tracy shook her head slowly. "This whole thing sounds crazy," she told him. "It would never work."

The two kittens raced across Josh's foot, and a small smile crept into his eyes. "I'm only doing it for my dad," he told her quietly. "He's been so sick and it would make him really happy if the whole family could be there, together."

Tracy pushed her own plate away. "Damnit,

Josh, that's not fair," she protested. Was she that transparent?

"What's not fair?" he asked, pretending not to understand her. "You don't want to make an old man happy?"

She got up from the table, and picked up Paddy's dish from the corner. "I can't just leave," she pointed out stubbornly. "What about the animals?"

"You said the kittens were leaving soon," he said. "Can't they go before Christmas?"

"But what about Paddy? I can't just leave him."

"Bring him along," Josh shrugged. "My dad loves dogs."

Tracy sighed as she poured some dry dog food into Paddy's dish and stirred in a spoonful of cat food. She put it on the floor and watched as Paddy wolfed the food down.

"It'd never work," she warned him. "I'm no good at acting. I can't pretend to be in love with you."

"Pretend I'm that stray animal you took in last night, then," he said, knowing that she was weakening. "And no one's going to pay that much attention to us. Besides my parents, Dan and his wife, Joan, and their three kids are coming in from San Francisco."

"And Monica," she added.

"Well, Monica and Charlie and their two kids live in town, and they will be around most of the time," he admitted. "It'll be a houseful and no one will be watching us. All you'll have to do is be there to relieve the pressure."

She sighed and sank back into her chair. She

was letting her attraction to him talk her into it, and that made her angry. "What about the payment you mentioned?" she asked, trying to show a tiny bit of backbone.

"How much do you want?" he asked with such efficiency that Tracy expected him to whip out his checkbook and pay her then and there. If nothing else, it effectively squashed any hopes that she might have had that he was attracted to her and was using this as an excuse to get to know her better.

"I don't know," Tracy cried, inexplicably disappointed. "I don't want anything. I want to be left alone to have a normal Christmas."

"Did you have plans?" he asked fearfully. "Are you going to see your own family?"

She shook her head, even though she knew that she ought to make use of the way out he presented her with. "No, my parents live in Florida now, and a recent transmission job wiped out my Christmas trip down there. I was just planning a quiet Christmas at home."

"How about if I pay for a trip down to see them?" he suggested quickly. "Whenever you want, and I'll even send you first class."

Tracy closed her eyes and leaned her head on her hands. "It just sounds so insane," she moaned. "I'd have a nervous breakdown before the first day was over."

"Bring your camera," he suggested. "They're predicting snow for Christmas, so you could get some great shots. And I heard that Jim Novak is looking for rural winter scenes for a special Sunday insert he's got planned for late January."

Tracy leaned back in her chair suddenly and

glared at him with real disgust. "You're despicable," she told him. "Utterly ruthless, with no conscience at all."

"But you'll do it?" he asked.

She nodded slowly. "I'll do it."

Chapter Three

JOSH AND TRACY left her apartment around noon
and drove down Foster Avenue to the Kennedy
Expressway. Tracy's suitcase and a bag of dog food
were in the trunk of Josh's BMW, while Paddy was
sound asleep in the backseat, snoring contentedly.

After passing through the industrial areas of
northwest Chicago on the expressway, they took
the Northwest Tollway, past O'Hare Airport and
the office complexes that surround it, and through
some of the more newly built-up suburbs. The lots
were larger and the houses newer than most in
Chicago, but to Tracy they lacked the charm and
individuality of some of the old neighborhoods in
the city. There were no interesting lines to capture
with a camera.

About ten miles past Woodfield Shopping Center, Josh got off the tollway and headed north on
Barrington Road. The countryside was far different
from that closer to Chicago. Patches were heavily
wooded, and the gentle hills and curves of the road
brought the ever-changing scenery to view. The
houses were large and spacious, and looked a part
of the landscape.

They turned onto Route 14 around one o'clock;
soon after, it began to snow lightly. Once through
Barrington, the road stayed close to the Chicago

and Northwestern Railroad tracks, so on their left was the steep incline up to the tracks. On their right, they passed such exciting sights as camper dealers and rustproofing shops. Fox River Grove had a castle perched on a hill overlooking the railroad tracks and the bitterly cold-looking Fox River to distinguish it. Cary had a small park with a lagoon, and Crystal Lake had one stoplight after another.

North of Crystal Lake, the countryside changed again. Suddenly, farmhouses appeared at the side of the road, surrounded by snow-covered empty fields. The atmosphere seemed more relaxed and unhurried, but with each passing minute Tracy grew more and more apprehensive. The whole masquerade was insane. There was no way they could pretend to care about each other, any more than Denise's old ring could pretend to be small enough to fit her finger.

Sixteen miles to Harvard. The green-and-white sign jumped out at her, and her stomach tightened with tension as she regretted ever agreeing to this. Josh was not particularly reassuring either, she thought, glancing resentfully at him. He had barely spoken two words to her since he had tossed her Denise's ring, before loading her things into his car. Tracy knew, though, that his silence was not caused by last-minute doubts. More likely, he had dismissed the whole thing from his mind.

Ten miles to Harvard. Tracy tried to be interested in the Plum Tree Golf Course to their left, but couldn't. She twisted her hands together nervously, wishing Josh would decide to turn back. More houses were gradually appearing, a sign of their proximity to a town that she noted with dis-

may. Suddenly, they came over a hill and she saw
Harvard spread out below them. Her mouth went
dry.

A large brown sign informed her that the Ro-
tary Club, the Lions Club, and many others welcomed her to Harvard, but even the appearance
of a McDonald's did little to reassure her. They
passed more houses, rather small and plain, but
the lots were large. A manufacturing plant loomed
on her right, its salmon-colored water tower huge
next to the low buildings near it.

"Will I have to be Denise?" she asked Josh
abruptly as they drove over a bumpy bridge that
crossed some railroad tracks.

He gave her a quick frown and slowed down to
negotiate an icy patch of road.

"I mean, will your parents be calling me Denise?" she explained.

"Why should they do that?" he snapped, im-
patient with her for some reason.

"Well, didn't you tell them about her when you
got engaged?" Tracy asked, conscious of her panic
rising every time he slowed the car slightly. "I
thought I was supposed to be taking her place."

"I don't remember what I told them," he
shrugged as they passed a sign advertising bingo at
St. Joseph's Church. "And I doubt that they do
either."

Obviously he had dismissed her worry as unimportant, but Tracy was not so easily relieved.
Her mother remembered everything about everyone she ever dated, even men Tracy had only mentioned briefly on the phone or in a letter. Somehow
she feared that Josh's mother would be the same

about her son's fiancée, and might be inclined to remember even such a little thing as her name.

Not really able to explain her fears, Tracy watched out the window as they drove north out of the town. Past the John Deere and International Harvester dealers, Josh turned right. The road went from smooth to bumpy to gravel, and then Josh turned left into a driveway. A faded red barn was off to their left, and a number of smaller gray buildings were scattered next to it, disappearing behind the large white farmhouse. It was a two-story, boxlike house with a wide front porch that looked bleak and forbidding. Maybe it was just the thick blanket of snow that covered the fields in every direction so that the house was the only sign of life in sight. Or maybe it was the wind that whipped across the frozen emptiness to chill her soul, but Tracy eyed the house warily.

"This is never going to work," she whispered, panic-stricken, only to find that Josh was already out of the car and coming around to open her door.

A tall woman with gray hair appeared on the porch of the house. She was wearing a blue print housedress that was covered with a bib apron and she had a black sweater pulled over that. Closing the door behind her, she called something to Josh. He waved with a smile as he opened Tracy's door. Tracy was about to make a last-minute plea that they abandon his plan when Paddy climbed over the seat and scrambled out the door.

Tracy made a mad dash for the dog, but he eluded her and raced over to the huge evergreens in front of the house to sniff at them happily. The woman came down the steps, interrupting Tracy's pursuit of Paddy. She was obviously Josh's mother, for she bore a striking resemblance to him in every way except her smile. Tracy doubted that Josh was capable of smiling with such warmth and welcome.

"Oh, it's so wonderful to meet you at last, Denise," Mrs. Rettinger sighed as she threw her arms around Tracy and hugged her warmly.

"It's Tracy, Mother," Josh noted offhandedly as he stopped behind them with the suitcases.

Mrs. Rettinger let go of Tracy slowly and gave her son a puzzled look. "I thought you told me her name was Denise," she said with a slight laugh.

"You must be getting old," he teased, leaning over to kiss her quickly on the cheek. "Tracy doesn't sound anything like Denise. What room are you giving her?" he asked as he climbed up the steps to the house.

His mother stared after him for a moment, then, giving Tracy a smile, she took her arm to lead her up the stairs. "Put her cases in your room for now," she told Josh while Tracy's heart stopped in astonishment. That was not part of the deal, she almost cried in angry protest, but Mrs. Rettinger went on. "Your father was sure that was where you'd want her, although Dan was under the impression you weren't even coming. We'll get the rooms sorted out later. Right now, I just want to get to know your Tracy."

Tracy feared her answering smile was rather forced as Paddy shuffled up the steps behind them. "I hope you don't mind that I brought my dog," she said dutifully.

"Oh, the more the merrier," Mrs. Rettinger laughed, unaware that Tracy's thoughts were preoccupied: she mentally berated herself for overlooking the fact that these days most engaged couples would share a room. Certainly Josh should have thought of it. Or had he? Her eyes narrowed suspiciously as they followed him into the house.

The house was as warm and welcoming as Mrs. Rettinger's smile. The large foyer that they stepped into had highly polished, golden brown floors and soft green walls. Off to one side, a wide staircase rose to the second floor. The steps were the same warm brown of the floor although a worn green rug ran down the center of them. The bannister was a deeper brown, held up by intricately carved posts, and decorated with a long rope of pine boughs that went up the stairs and along the balcony that overlooked the front door. Held in place with large, red satin bows, the pine boughs made the room look beautiful and smell even better.

"How beautiful!" Tracy sighed while she handed Josh her coat. "I'm so glad I brought my camera."

Josh gave her a strange look as he hung up their coats. "I'll take the bags upstairs," he said and moved toward the stairs.

"Did you want to freshen up?" Mrs. Rettinger asked Tracy as she watched Josh depart. "Or would you like something hot to drink? It's several hours until dinner."

Deciding to tackle Josh about the rooms later, Tracy picked up the bag of dog food from the floor. "I'd love something hot," she agreed.

Mrs. Rettinger led her and Paddy through a doorway under the stairs and into the kitchen. It was a big room, longer than it was wide, with the appliances at one end and a large table covered with baking utensils at the other. Windows along the far wall let in a breathtaking view of gentle, snow-covered hills behind the house. There was no definite color scheme as in the highly decorated farm kitchens pictured in magazines; rather there was just a general feeling of warmth and belonging that felt like home. Tracy loved it.

"Where can I put Paddy's things?" she asked, turning away with reluctance from her inspection of the room. "Oh, and I need to refrigerate his insulin."

Mrs. Rettinger had been checking something fragrant in the oven and looked up in surprise. "Paddy's a diabetic?" she asked with a laugh. "Well, what a surprise! Did Josh tell you his dad is also? John'll like having someone to commiserate with when the cookies are passed around." She nodded toward a door past the stove. "Put his things in the pantry, there," she said, taking two cups down from the mix-matched collection on a shelf near the sink. "And why don't you leave his water dish in the corner over by the table? That's where our dogs always had theirs since it's out of the way."

While Tracy fixed Paddy a dish of water, Mrs. Rettinger cleared some of the baking things off one end of the worn wooden table and put down the cups. "What will you have? Coffee, tea, or hot chocolate? I've got hot water and can make any of them."

"Hot chocolate, please," Tracy said. Paddy came over and took a drink of his water and then allowed her to scratch him behind his ears before he found a place near the windows to lie down.

Tracy straightened up to find Mrs. Rettinger

watching her. "You know, you're very different from the way I had imagined you," she admitted as she opened a couple of the gaily painted tins that were on the table and put a variety of Christmas cookies on a plate. "Have you done much performing?"

"I beg your pardon?" Tracy murmured as she walked over to her place at the table. Had Mrs. Rettinger seen through this mockery of an engagement already?

"Josh said you were a singer," Mrs. Rettinger said, a puzzled look on her face. "However, he also said your name was Denise."

Tracy sat down with a sigh. So much for Josh's assurances that no one would remember anything. "I'm not an actress. I'm a photographer. I work with Josh."

Mrs. Rettinger pushed over the plate of cookies and Tracy helped herself to one shaped like a flower with a candied cherry center. "So who's Denise?" she asked with a suspicious twinkle in her eye.

"Uh, Denise was someone Josh knew a while ago," Tracy said lamely, taking a quick drink of the hot chocolate.

Mrs. Rettinger smiled knowingly. "Before he met you," she said.

Tracy nodded and took another cookie. "These are really good," she said brightly. "My mom used to bake a lot of Christmas cookies, but we never had anything like these."

Josh came into the kitchen, and Tracy smiled at him in relief. Now he could field his mother's questions. Something about the look Mrs. Rettinger gave her, though, made her suspect that the other woman had interpreted her smile differently.

"Make yourself some coffee and join us," his mother told him as Paddy got up to greet Josh. "Tracy's been telling me how you dumped Denise when you two met."

Tracy nearly choked on her hot chocolate as Josh turned slowly to look at her. He raised one eyebrow expressively, then finished making his coffee. "I take it from your gleeful expression that you are not shocked," he said mildly, coming to join them at the table.

"Of course not," his mother scoffed. She offered him the plate of cookies, and put it back by Tracy after he had taken a handful. "I think it's terribly romantic and not like you at all. It's obvious that Tracy has done you a world of good already."

Tracy bit back a laugh at the expression of irritation on Josh's face and smiled sweetly when Mrs. Rettinger turned to her. "When is the wedding going to be?" Josh's mother asked her.

It was Josh's turn to laugh at her discomfort, which his eyes did as he finished the last of his cookies.

"We haven't decided yet," Tracy admitted, hit with a flash of inspiration. "We just got engaged and I haven't even had time to get my ring fixed." She held out her left hand where Denise's diamond lay crookedly on her finger. "Josh wanted it to be a surprise and didn't take me with him to have it sized," she went on in a gushy, breathless voice.

Josh stopped laughing and frowned at her while his mother admired the ring. "I can't get over it," she laughed. "You must have him bewitched. He's always been far too practical and predictable.''

Tracy smiled. Voices were suddenly heard from behind the house. She turned to look through the window at a swarm of children around two men with a Christmas tree.

''Oh, they're back already,'' Josh's mother said in surprise, then explained to Tracy: ''Dan and Charlie took the kids to cut down the tree from a stand of pines on the north edge of the property.''

''You mean you grow your own Christmas trees?'' she sighed. ''That's really something.''

Mrs. Rettinger went over to the sink and rinsed her cup out before leaving it in the dish drainer. ''It's too bad you weren't here earlier. You could have gone with them.'' She wiped her hands on her apron. ''I'd better go see how big that thing is before they drag it into the living room and find it doesn't fit. Help yourselves to more cookies and drinks,'' she added, disappearing into a mud room off the kitchen. A sudden blast of cold air followed the sound of the outside door being closed.

Tracy watched them drag the Christmas tree around the side of the house for a minute before she realized that this was the time to tackle Josh about the rooms. She turned around to find him reading a local newspaper that he had found on the table.

''I think we'd better get this room situation straightened out now,'' she said warningly, determined to make her opinion in the matter quite clear.

He looked up from the paper, a frown creasing his forehead. ''What room situation?'' he asked.

Tracy went back to the table, choosing to stand

behind her chair so that she had the advantage of height for once. "I have no intention of sharing your room while we're here," she informed him.

"I don't recall ever inviting you to," he retorted calmly.

Tracy was not fooled by his easy manner. "Yeah, I noticed how hard you argued with your mother about it," she said coldly. "Maybe I agreed to help you out without thinking things through first, but I wasn't born yesterday. I can see what you're after." She folded her arms across her chest and glared at him fiercely.

Josh's voice stayed quiet, but his eyes became hard and cold. "Believe me, if I'm after anything, it certainly isn't you." His eyes raked her small figure scathingly. "The world must be filled with desperate men if you're accosted as constantly as your manner indicates, but I'm definitely not that hard up. My tastes run to something a bit more sophisticated than blue jeans, homeless kittens, and wide-eyed awe over Christmas trees." He drank the rest of his coffee quickly and rose to his feet. "If you'll excuse me, I think I'll take a walk."

Refusing to show the hurt that his words had caused, Tracy continued to glare at him as he stalked over to the mud room. He stopped at the doorway and turned to face her again. "Oh, by the way, your suitcase is in my mother's sewing room at the end of the hall. All the other rooms seemed occupied, so I thought you could use the sofa bed in there." Without waiting for a reply, he donned a worn plaid jacket that was probably his father's and went outside.

Once the sound of the door closing died away, Tracy let herself sink slowly into her chair. She knew she ought to be furious with him, but she felt more pain than anger. She had never thought she was sophisticated, nor had even wanted to be, but she didn't think that her values were so immature as to be worthy of ridicule.

Blinking back the tears that had formed suddenly in her eyes, she chided herself severely. Why should she expect Josh to become a reasonable, polite human being just because she had agreed to help him? It would serve him right if she packed up Paddy and left, letting him explain the sudden disappearance of his fiancée; but she knew she wouldn't. It was because this was a much better place to spend Christmas than her apartment, she assured herself blithely; but, deep down, she knew better. She was much too softhearted to abandon Josh, even if he was insufferably arrogant and rude.

Much laughter and cold air announced the arrival of the Christmas tree and the selection committee at the front door. With a sigh, Tracy rose to her feet to go meet more of Josh's family. She wondered if they'd think it odd that Josh had gone out, leaving her to meet them by herself. Squeals from the children told her that Paddy had already gone ahead, and she hurried after him. The dog was certainly more fun than Josh, so maybe they wouldn't notice he wasn't around.

Josh looked up from the chessboard and glanced around the living room, thinking that it had not changed much since he was a child. It was a large room, with a high patterned plaster ceiling surrounded by carved wooden moldings. The walls were white and covered with bookshelves between the tall windows and wide fireplace. Individual pieces of furniture had been replaced, but they all had the same comfortable appearance that gave the room its welcoming air.

The Christmas tree was being put up in the window at the front of the house, as usual. Josh watched as Tracy and Dan strung the lights on the Christmas tree. Dan's wife, Joan, heavily pregnant with their fourth child, was directing their efforts from the floor.

"She certainly fits right in," Mr. Rettinger said quietly as he moved his knight and captured one of Josh's pawns.

"Mmmm," Josh muttered noncommittally, turning his attention back to the game. He knew his father was right, but the knowledge bothered him slightly. He retaliated by moving his bishop purposefully across the board.

"Aha!" his father cried happily, his voice surprisingly strong for his frail appearance. "That was a dumb move!" He took Josh's bishop with a rook and a gloating smile. "I always like to play chess with a man in love. He can never quite concentrate."

Josh scowled at him, and then stared down at the board. He could hardly argue the point, so he renewed his determination to win. Unfortunately, when the sound of Tracy's laughter floated toward him, he could not stop his eyes from seeking her out. Nor could he force them away from the sight of her slim figure, neatly encased in designer jeans and a close-fitting red velour top, as she stretched to loop the string of lights over a top branch. His father's quiet chuckle brought him back to their chess game in a hurry.

There was no denying the fact that his family had warmly accepted her and that the usual restraint accompanying his visits was gone. Of course, a little less enthusiasm might have been preferable. All during dinner, his father had regaled Tracy with ridiculous stories of Josh's childhood, while his mother had promised her a number of family recipes that she simply would "have to have."

Josh found their wholehearted acceptance a trifle annoying and had to remind himself several times that his father's ill health had necessitated the deception. What was even more annoying, though, was the fact that he was enjoying her company just as much as anyone and had even caught himself looking for excuses to be with her. Luckily, they would not be here long.

After careful deliberation, Josh moved his queen. There was no immediate pouncing; his father frowned thoughtfully and studied the board before his next move. Josh allowed himself to relax slightly.

Dan and Joan seemed to enjoy Tracy's company also and seemed more relaxed with her than they did with him. But then, they were very close to Monica and Charlie and always seemed to view him as some sort of threat. As if he'd ever want to get back together with Monica! Josh thought with disgust.

His father moved his knight again, and Josh countered with his knight. It probably was just as well that Denise was not around. He couldn't see his parents relaxing much around her.

Josh turned and saw Tracy sitting cross-legged on the floor with Matt and Mike, Dan's seven-year-old twins. They were noisily stringing popcorn while Paddy rested his head on Tracy's leg, sorrowfully watching the popcorn disappear. She was telling them about the various animals that she had kept for the animal shelter, and they looked enthralled. No, he thought as he went back to his game. This definitely was not Denise's scene.

They had almost finished decorating the tree and Josh had lost several more chess pieces when the front door opened.

"Hello, hello, everybody," a short, pudgy blonde in a white fur coat called out. Her curly hair delicately peeped out from under her matching fur hat and framed her round face. She would have looked rather colorless had it not been for her rosy cheeks and startlingly blue eyes. Charlie and their two little girls hovered behind her.

The blonde spotted Tracy hanging a string of popcorn with Mike and floated over toward her. "You must be Tracy," she sighed in a breathless voice as she threw her arms around the surprised young woman. "Charlie and the girls told me all about you."

Tracy murmured something, looking rather uncomfortable with Monica's appearance. She probably expected someone like Denise, Josh thought; instinctively he rose to his feet and walked over to Tracy's side. Monica was very good at appearing small and fragile, although she was anything but.

Tracy seemed surprised when he put his arm protectively around her shoulders, but he kept his eyes on Monica. "Looks like you've put on a little weight, Monica," he said lightly.

"Josh!" Mrs. Rettinger protested.

But Monica just shook her head with a smile. "I

should have known you'd notice that extra pound or two," she sighed.

It looked more like twenty or thirty, he thought, his lips tightening with irritation at the way she manipulated his words to her advantage. He had forgotten just how expert she was at that.

Charlie had followed her across the room. After a quick nervous glance at Josh, he offered to take her coat.

"Oh, how silly of me," she laughed with embarrassment, but Josh was not fooled. Monica never forgot anything. The question was, whom had she wanted to impress with the attractive picture she presented when wearing it?

Under the coat was a lacy white blouse and a long red velvet skirt that was far dressier than Mrs. Rettinger's navy dress, Joan's green pantsuit, or Tracy's jeans and top. Not that it appeared to bother Monica, though, for she always had considered herself a fashion expert with an image to uphold. Apparently being the wife of the vice-president of the Harvard State Bank was closer to that image than the wife of a newspaper reporter ever was.

After handing her coat and hat to Charlie with a fond smile, Monica straightened the lace cuffs on her blouse and then put one fat little hand on Josh's arm.

"How are you, Josh?" she asked, her voice filled with regretful concern. "I mean, really."

"I'm just fine, thank you," he said briskly. "Really and truly," he added mockingly.

"I certainly would be fine if I were going to marry someone like Tracy," his father stated loudly with a sly wink at Tracy.

Tracy smiled back at him, and Monica looked quite injured. "Oh, I never meant that he wasn't. I've always hoped that he would find someone else to be happy with," she assured everyone in a pouty little voice.

"We know that, darling." Joan hurried over to take her arm. "Why don't we leave the tree-trimming to the children and make some eggnog?"

With relief, Josh watched them leave the room. He never could take Monica for very long, and wondered why he was the only one who saw through her act. He suddenly needed some restful company. "I think Tracy and I'll take a walk," he announced to no one in particular; he took the end of the popcorn string from Tracy's hand and gave it to Dan's five-year-old daughter, Karen.

Then, taking Tracy's arm, he led her out of the room. Paddy ran along behind them.

"I thought you were playing chess," she reminded him as they entered the foyer.

He shrugged. "This way I won't actually lose."

After helping her into her coat and putting his on, they went outside. Paddy raced across the freshly fallen snow, snuffling around with his nose, burrowing a trail as he tracked down unseen dangers.

The yard was lit by the lights from the house, which reflected on the glistening blanket of snow. It was peaceful and quiet, with no sounds of traffic or the glare of street lights to mar the beauty. It was a perfect setting for romance, and Josh wondered if escaping Monica had been the real reason he had wanted to come out here with Tracy. He suddenly made a snowball and threw it for Paddy, who ran around where it landed, searching frantically among the disintegrated pieces.

What the hell was he doing? Josh asked himself angrily. He could not get involved with someone like Tracy. Perfect as she might seem for the role of his fiancée, she was quite definitely not his type. So she was cute and could make his body ache to hold her; there was a bit more to a relationship than that. He had better quit his stupid daydreaming and face reality.

"Won't it look strange that we left as soon as Monica and Charlie came?" Tracy broke into his thoughts to ask.

Josh had bent down to make another snowball, fighting his attraction to her with activity; he looked up at her words. "I'm supposed to prefer your company, remember?"

"Yeah, I know that, but it seemed like you were afraid to stay in there with her," Tracy argued.

Josh stood up. She was too nice, too friendly, he thought, and impossible to ignore. He could fight the attraction better if she'd just keep her distance. "Maybe I couldn't stand being in there with all those kids," he said curtly.

That surprised her. "You don't like kids?"

"Not particularly," he admitted as he turned away to throw the snowball for Paddy. "That's why Denise and I were so well suited. I'm not exactly the Daddy type, and that was fine with her."

"Was that why you and Monica were divorced?" Tracy asked curiously.

Josh began throwing snowballs at a huge old tree down the yard from them so he appeared detached and unconcerned. It wasn't that the question made him uncomfortable, for his feelings for

Monica were long dead. No, it was the necessity to kill the feelings for Tracy that were starting to grow. It seemed wrong to destroy something that felt so right, but he knew it had to be done.

"Partly that," he said, deliberately nonchalant. "She was pretty much like you—reeking with love for everyone." He wasn't watching her but he could sense her stiffen.

"You don't seem very complimentary." Her voice sounded forced.

He shrugged and then turned to face her. "Hey, normally I avoid women like you like the plague, but I knew the folks would be much more impressed with you than with Denise," he pointed out. "And they really like you. Hiring you to be my fiancée was probably the smartest move I've made in a long time."

It was hard to judge her feelings because the dim light hid her face from him, but her voice was crisp and businesslike. "Well, I think I had better get back in and earn my pay," she said a tad too brightly. "Besides, Paddy's feet bother him if he's out in the snow too long." She turned toward the house, calling the dog.

"I'm going to move my car in back," Josh called to her as Paddy climbed up the steps behind her. Standing in the brighter light on the porch, she nodded, then pulled open the door and went inside.

Josh walked slowly over to his car, fingering the keys in his pocket thoughtfully. She was a nice kid, and he hated to hurt her feelings like that, but it really was for the best. No matter how you looked at it, Denise was much more his type than Tracy would ever be.

Chapter Four

A COLD, WET NOSE woke Tracy up sometime during the night.

"What do you want, Paddy?" she sighed, reaching for her watch. It seemed as if she had just gotten to bed after the midnight church service they had gone to, but it was already 6:30 in the morning. She had a pretty good idea of why Paddy was waking her up. "Okay, okay," she yawned and pushed the blanket away.

It had been cozy and warm under the down comforter that Mrs. Rettinger had given her, and Tracy was unprepared for the chill in the room. She hurried into the furry red robe that her mother had given her last Christmas and pulled on a pair of thick white socks that would have to serve for the slippers she had forgotten.

"Let's go, Paddy," she whispered and led him out into the hallway. They passed a tarnished mirror at the top of the stairs that reflected her mussed hair and sleepy eyes. Hardly competition for Monica, she thought with a wry smile. But then, who was competing with her? Who even wanted to compete with her?

The house was cold and dark, but Tracy found her way to the kitchen with no trouble and turned on the lights. The room was especially cozy when it was dark outside. She led Paddy across to the mud-room door and let him out.

"Now don't wander off," she called after him warningly. "I'm not coming out there to get you."

"My, my, how selfish of you!"

Tracy spun around to see Josh leaning against the kitchen doorway. He was wearing a navy robe trimmed with burgundy-and-beige stripes on the sleeves, and from the look of his bare feet and legs, little else.

Tracy shivered when she saw him. "Aren't you freezing?" she asked.

He smiled. "And I thought that was a shiver of excitement at the sight of me," he teased her. "No, I'm not cold, and I'm sure you're not, either. Not bundled up like that. I hope my parents don't see you," he went on. "I don't think it would be good for my image. I like to think I attract the black negligee type."

Tracy glanced out the window to keep an eye on Paddy. "Negligees don't exactly keep you warm," she pointed out. Paddy came up to the door and she went to let him back in.

"Maybe not, but they could inspire some man to take over the job."

Tracy frowned at him over her shoulder. "No, thanks. I'll stick with my robe."

Josh looked surprised at the bitterness in her voice. "That's a pretty sweeping statement for someone who must be all of twenty-two," he said, filling the teapot with water and putting it on the stove.

"I'm twenty-seven," she noted, pulling clumps of snow from Paddy's feet. "And quite satisfied with things as they are, thank you."

She had not forgotten his curt reminder last evening that she was being paid to play a part, and she was determined to keep everything very impersonal between them. It was true that she found his family enjoyable, and was finding herself more and more attracted to him, but he had quite clearly defined their relationship last night. She was not about to risk such a verbal thrashing again. He could play whatever little games he liked with his suggestive remarks, but she would have no part of it.

"Just your dogs, your cats, and your camera, right?" he mocked her with a laugh. "I find that hard to believe."

"Why? Denise obviously put her career ahead of you," she pointed out and picked up the disposable syringe that she had brought downstairs with her. "Am I so different?"

"Lord, yes," he laughed with honest amusement. He took down two cups from a shelf near the sink and got the jar of instant coffee from a nearby cabinet. "Denise did not have the mothering urge so strongly that she had to take in abandoned animals until she found some man to marry."

Tracy had opened the refrigerator to get Paddy's insulin, but slammed the door shut and spun around to face him. "You couldn't be more wrong," she informed him angrily. "I've tried both routes and, believe me, I prefer the animals over a husband any day!"

The surprise on Josh's face gave Tracy only slight satisfaction. Her marriage to David was not something that she wanted to discuss with him, and she regretted letting her anger carry her away. She turned away from him to fill the syringe, hoping against hope that he would be polite enough to change the subject.

"I didn't know that you had been married," he said slowly. The water had come to a boil and he poured it into the two cups, stirring in the instant coffee as he watched her.

"It's not a subject that usually comes up in the course of our conversations," she pointed out, cleaning a spot on Paddy's side with an antiseptic wipe. Then she lifted up the loose skin slightly and slid the needle in, pushing in the plunger to release the insulin under his skin. "We only work at the same paper. It's not as if we were friends or anything, so why should you know anything about me?"

Her eyes on Paddy, Tracy missed the frown that suddenly crossed Josh's features. After removing the needle, she wiped the site again before straightening up. "Actually, I doubt that I've discussed my marriage with anyone at work," she said, hoping her voice clearly reflected her desire to close the discussion.

"What happened? Was he fooling around with other women?" Josh asked, ignoring her unspoken message.

Tracy's lips twisted in irritation. "Did it ever occur to you that I might not want to discuss it?"

"I told you about Monica," he pointed out reasonably, carrying the two cups of coffee to the table. "Do you take milk or sugar in your coffee?"

She shook her head as she sat down at the table with a sigh. "No, he wasn't exactly 'fooling around.' "

Josh had been about to take a drink of coffee but

stopped with his cup in midair. "How do you 'not exactly' fool around?" he asked.

Tracy shrugged her shoulders, then put her elbows on the table, running her fingers through her hair. "I mean, he was after a while, but, in a way, it was my fault."

"Don't tell me," he snapped. "Another guilt-ridden female blaming herself because her husband was an asshole. Somehow I thought better of you."

"David was not an asshole!" she exclaimed, sitting up straighter so that she could glare across the table at him. "What happened wasn't anybody's fault."

She didn't like the disbelieving look on his face, and stood up, walking over to the large window to gaze out. It was just beginning to get light and the kitchen was losing that safe, cocoonlike feeling.

Her voice was quiet when she spoke again. "David was in his early thirties when he became editor of the paper I was working on. He wasn't a real ambitious guy, and was quite satisfied with his present job. All he wanted was a home and a family." She turned to face him with a wry grimace on her face. "The home part was easy; it was the family part that wrecked us."

She hadn't expected his eyes to soften with sympathy the way they did, and she came slowly back to the table, certain for some reason that he was not going to blame her as others had. She sat down again.

"After we had been married for about a year and a half, and I still wasn't pregnant, I went to the doctor," she said quietly as she stared down at her hands that were clutching the cup of coffee. "I began to live two weeks at a time: from ovulation to menstruation back to ovulation; but nothing the doctors did seemed to work. Finally, I was hospitalized for some tests and they learned that my Fallopian tubes were blocked by scar tissue. I had had an infection sometime and it had cleared up by itself, but had left a little present for me. One tube was totally blocked, the other might as well have been. My chances of getting pregnant were almost nonexistent, the doctor said."

She suddenly stopped talking, wondering why in the world she had confided so much to him. It had taken her a long time, but she had managed to regain her confidence in herself. She didn't need his assurance, or anyone else's, that the inability to conceive made her less of a woman.

"Is that when he began to see other women?" Josh asked quietly.

Tracy looked up at him and tried to smile. "Oh, he was fair about it," she acknowledged, her humor coming out more bitterly than she intended. "Cindy and I were given equal chances. But she got pregnant first, so it was bye-bye, Tracy." She tried to smile at him again.

"What a fool!" Josh muttered, shaking his head. "That's not what you base a marriage on."

"Maybe not, but they were very happy," Tracy was quick to point out. "The last time I saw them they had the house, two cars, and the average one-point-eight kids."

"One-point-eight?" he asked. "She was pregnant again?"

Tracy nodded, her mouth unable to form the smile this time. "Of course, that was over a year ago; by now it could be different.'' Her voice died away as she tried to regain control.

"This is really stupid," she said in embarrassment after a long moment. Her voice was shaky and she had wiped a few tears from her cheeks. "It's been almost three years since we were divorced, and I really am used to the fact. I shouldn't be getting so upset."

"Maybe you still care about him," Josh suggested quietly.

"David?" she asked in astonishment. "Oh, no, it was much harder to accept the fact that I can't have kids than the divorce. David became rather incidental, I'm afraid." She took a long sip of coffee, to give her thoughts time to clear. "It's not quite like admitting that you can't sing, you know," she told him, back to staring at her hands. "But I'm still me. I'm still a good photographer, I still like animals. . . ."

"Still a soft touch," he interrupted.

She looked up at him, smiling a more honest smile. "Yeah," she agreed. "That's me."

The silence that filled the room was more companionable as they drank their coffee slowly.

"You know what I think?" Josh asked her suddenly, putting down his cup.

She looked up at him.

"I don't think the bastard ever cared about you," he said. "Oh, maybe he was fond of you, but if he really loved you, he couldn't have let you go."

Tracy just stared at him.

"If you really love someone, you're willing to make compromises and adjust what you want," he went on. "You can't leave them, no matter what."

Paddy suddenly nudged Tracy's arm and she looked down at him in surprise. "I almost forgot about you," she told him, scratching his head as she got to her feet.

She measured out the dog food into Paddy's dish and put it on the floor, watching absently while the dog began to eat. Josh's words kept running through her mind. She had never tried to analyze David's feelings toward her. Maybe he hadn't really cared for her as she had cared for him.

That thought did not lessen the echo of the agonies she had suffered when she had learned that she probably would never have a child. She had felt so worthless, such a failure, that David's leaving had been inevitable. She couldn't blame him for wanting a real woman for a wife.

It had taken her years to accept herself as a woman after that devastation, years of pain and doubt that kept coming back like the jealousy she felt at the sight of a pregnant woman. Even now, after she felt that she had conquered all of her doubts, she wasn't certain that she should have confided in Josh. Could she trust him not to use them against her in some way?

"Why don't you go up and change?" Josh said, interrupting her thoughts. "I'm going to have another cup of coffee, so I can let Paddy out when he's done."

Tracy just stared at him blankly for a minute. She had forgotten that he was even in the room with her. "Okay, thanks," she said slowly. "I think I could use a little time to get back in the spirit of this masquerade." Was it her imagination, she wondered as she walked toward the door, or was he actually being considerate?

"Hey, Tracy," Josh called to her just before she left the room.

She stopped and turned around.

He raised his coffee cup up in the air as for a toast. "Merry Christmas," he said quietly.

A smile spread slowly over Tracy's face. "Merry Christmas," she replied.

Tracy felt much more alive after a leisurely bath in a deep old tub with feet that resided in the bathroom across the hall from her room. She put on her makeup with care and fluffed her soft brown curls so that they framed her face attractively.

Although she was vaguely sorry that she had told Josh about her marriage and her own condition, Tracy knew exactly why she had done it. She had been angry at his insinuations, but she could have handled them without baring her innermost fears and insecurities. No, her reasons were more complicated than that.

She had this compulsion to blurt out the truth every time she found herself attracted to someone. It was as if, in spite of all her brave thoughts and assurances, she couldn't really believe that any man would want her. Not if they knew the truth about her. She had to put them to the test.

Of course, her dire expectations had come true a number of times. She had become slightly involved with several men since her divorce. However, before any real feelings could develop, she told them that she couldn't have children. Most of the men were sympathetic and kind, but did not hang around long after that.

Tracy had tried to convince herself that she was only being honest. She wasn't going to build a relationship on a lie; but it was far more than that. She desperately wanted to be close to someone again. In spite of her bravado, the dogs and cats were hardly a satisfactory substitute for a warm and loving relationship with a man. The trouble was, she was so terribly afraid to risk loving someone again that she usually made sure that she destroyed any relationship before it had a chance to hurt her.

Even though Josh had not shown any attraction toward her, she had felt her own interest stirring. That was why she had told him the truth. Then he would follow the pattern set by the others: polite sympathy and quiet withdrawal. There would be no more flirting or suggestive remarks. She would be alone again; but she would not have let herself fantasize about what might have been between them.

Tracy realized suddenly that she could hear voices coming from downstairs. She looked at her watch to discover that it was past eight o'clock, and it was quite apparent that no one in this house slept late on Christmas morning.

She quickly slipped into her cream satin blouse with the high ruffled collar and long full sleeves. Her deep red velveteen slacks emphasized her slender legs, and made her look taller, she thought, while the matching red vest called attention to her full breasts. She put on a pair of thin golden circle earrings that dangled amid her curls, and stepped into her shoes.

After slipping Denise's ring onto her finger, Tracy picked up two foil-wrapped presents tied with red ribbons. As Josh's fiancée, she could hardly appear at Christmas without gifts, but she was not quite as confident of her choices as she had been two days ago. She wished that she had talked to Josh about them this morning, but then she had had other things on her mind.

With a sigh, she turned to the door, ready to go downstairs. She was mentally back in her role, and knew she could perform the masquerade quite adequately. Of course it would be easier now that that was the only thing she had to worry about, she told herself as she went out into the hallway. Since Josh knew about her, any flirting he did would be in the presence of others, for the sake of the masquerade. Her heart would be safe.

She walked past the tarnished mirror at the top of the stairs, never realizing how foolish her words sounded when compared to her lovely body and loving ways.

All of Josh's family was gathered in the large living room when Tracy entered, but she was relieved to see that Monica and her family were not present. There was coffee, tea, and orange juice on the hutch by the far wall, along with a tray of small sweet rolls. Mrs. Rettinger was encouraging people to help themselves, while Dan and Joan's children were searching through the presents piled under the tree.

When Josh spotted her, he put down his coffee cup. '' 'Bout time you came down, lazybones,'' he teased. He came over to her and bent to plant a lingering kiss on her lips. ''Merry Christmas, darling.''

Tracy's eyes widened; the warmth and gentleness of his lips had surprised her, even though she knew the kiss had just been for show. ''Merry Christmas,'' she repeated. Her voice sounded annoyingly soft and breathless.

Josh kept his arm possessively around her shoulders as he led her over to the hutch. "That thundering herd over there is anxious to start opening presents," he told her with a nod toward the kids. "So you'd better get yourself some sustenance."

"Merry Christmas, Tracy," Mrs. Rettinger smiled at her and leaned over to kiss her cheek. "Shall I put the presents under the tree for you while you fix yourself something to eat? The kids like to play Santa Claus and pass them all out." She took the gifts, but Tracy had no time to watch her place them under the tree, as Josh's father came over to greet her.

"You've got the right idea, son," Mr. Rettinger laughed, looking at Tracy with an appreciative gleam in his eye. "Let your mother take all those other presents; you've got Tracy. She's the kind of gorgeously wrapped gift I'd want under my tree."

Josh laughed and tightened his hold on Tracy's shoulders. "Keep away, Father. I saw her first."

Tracy joined their laughter even though she felt far from it. Josh's proximity was disturbing as he held her closely against his side, and it became far worse when he moved suddenly, his arms encircling her tightly as he stepped behind her. Laughing and talking to his father, he seemed barely aware of the fact that he was crushing her breasts beneath his arms and that her back was pressed tightly against his chest.

The tangy scent of his aftershave stirred her senses, and Tracy fought hard to remember that his show of affection was just an act. It was almost impossible to keep in mind, though, with the firm muscles of his thighs pressing against her. The protective strength of his arms seemed to wrap her in a sensuous cocoon that threatened to overcome the barriers that surrounded her heart.

Quite relieved when his father handed her a cup of coffee, Tracy moved out of the delicious circle of Josh's arms. His embrace had no right to be so comfortable, not when it was all a masquerade, she thought irritably. But she took her cup of coffee with a smile and allowed Josh to lead her over to a place on a love seat, not revealing any sign of the uneasiness that she felt inside.

Mike and Matt were soon ripping the paper off an electric-train set while Karen was unwrapping a doll. Mrs. Rettinger got a pink satin robe from Dan and Joan; her husband received a navy-blue cardigan sweater. Josh gave the two of them a new stereo.

It was ridiculous, Tracy told herself as she laughed and talked with the others and said all the proper exclamations over their gifts, but she was far more conscious of Josh's arm resting lightly across her shoulders than of anything else. When his thumb began to move gently back and forth in a slow, rhythmic caress, she was torn between a desire to pull away from him and a wish to succumb to the invitation of intimacy that his touch seemed to offer.

Luckily, her good sense prevailed and she remembered the reason for her presence before making a fool of herself. With what she fervently hoped was a natural smile, she leaned forward to pick up her coffee cup from the low table before her.

Josh seemed rather amused by her tactics, but was distracted by the arrival of Mike and Matt with a stack of presents for the two of them. Tracy noticed uneasily that her gift for Josh was in among them, and wished that she had had a chance to warn him about it. Surely, she worried, he would realize it was just part of the masquerade and not any wish on her part for a real relationship between them.

"Oh, Tracy, how marvelous!" Mrs. Rettinger cried. Tracy turned to discover that Josh's mother had opened the gift that she had brought for her and was holding up the framed photograph of Josh for the others to see. "Doesn't it look just like him?"

"Photographs usually do, Mother," Josh pointed out dryly.

Oh, Lord, Tracy thought. She should have warned him about that, too.

"Not yours," his father laughed as Mrs. Rettinger passed the picture over for him to see. "You're even less photogenic than I am." With a pleased smile, he looked down at the picture of his son, then back up at Tracy. "However did you get him to pose so naturally for you?"

"He didn't exactly pose," Tracy admitted, sensing Josh's displeasure quite strongly. For a moment she had regretted deciding to enlarge one of the photos she'd taken that afternoon on the roof but, seeing the happiness on his parents' faces, she was suddenly glad. They were obviously delighted with the gift, so what did it matter if he was angry? To prove her point, she glanced at him defiantly, only to find him watching her in a strange, speculative way.

"Aren't you going to open your presents?" Karen asked, obviously puzzled that someone could have a pile of presents and not be dying to open them.

"Sure," Tracy said, turning away from Josh to smile at his niece. She picked up the small package on the top, but Josh suddenly took it out of her hand.

"Open that last," he said when she frowned at him.

Dan laughed and made some remark about saving the best for last, but Tracy was too curious to pay much attention. She pretended to be interested only in the brightly colored scarf from Dan and Joan, even though her eyes kept straying to the box held lightly in Josh's hand. It was getting harder and harder to remember that they were both acting a part; not for the first time, she regretted agreeing to his insane suggestion.

With renewed determination to remain unmoved, Tracy opened up the Rettingers' gift. It was a traveling set of three small quilted bags. One unrolled with pockets for jewelry, another was for makeup, and the last was rectangular with stiff sides for carrying delicate things.

"It's so hard to buy for someone you don't know," Mrs. Rettinger said apologetically when Tracy was silent.

"Oh, it's lovely," Tracy assured her quickly. She could not explain that her silence had been due to a sudden wave of guilt that she was taking gifts that she did not deserve. The fact that she had brought gifts did little to ease her conscience.

Josh put her small present out of her reach and proceeded to open a long, white silk scarf from Dan. Somehow Tracy could not see him using something like that. Her skepticism must have been evident, for he suddenly looked up at her and they exchanged an amused glance.

Next he opened up a set of books from his parents and then a new robe that was exactly like the one he had been wearing that morning.

"But that's—" she began, then stopped, realizing it would be rude to let his mother know it was just like his old one.

Josh laughed at the look on her face. "Tracy doesn't want you to know this is just like my old robe," he told his mother with a laugh that grew louder when he saw Tracy's red face. "That's all right, darling," he said with a great show of affection. "That other was getting worn."

Tracy could have killed him for implying an intimacy that did not exist, even though she knew that everyone else supposed that it did. She relented slightly when he handed her the small present.

Her curiosity getting the best of her, Tracy pulled off the wrapping to find a plain white box. Inside was a cameo brooch. It was obviously old, for the clasp was strange, but the gold setting had been highly polished and the tiny pearls that encircled it were gleaming.

"Oh, it's beautiful, Josh," she breathed. "I've never had anything like this." Finally dragging her eyes away from it, she looked up at him. Her blue eyes were sparkling and there was a glow of excitement about her that he had never seen before.

"I'm glad you like it," he said quietly. He looked down into her eyes and, for a moment, Tracy forgot about their masquerade. She forgot that they were both playing a part and thought she could almost see care and concern in his eyes.

"Why don't you put it on?" Mrs. Rettinger asked. "It'll look lovely on your blouse."

Tracy broke the spell that held their eyes and turned toward the older woman, grateful that she brought reality back. However beautiful Josh's gift was it carried no deep meanings with it. Certainly no emotions other than gratitude.

She forced herself to keep the same bemused expression on her face as she pinned the brooch to her collar.

"It looks as if it were made for that blouse," Joan said. Her voice seemed rather quiet and faraway, and Tracy shook herself mentally. She was not some star-struck teenager who went into a daze over a gift or a man.

"I must have been psychic when I bought this outfit," Tracy laughed. "Thank you so much, Josh darling," she forced herself to say. Then she leaned over to kiss his lips lightly. There, she thought. I can play this game as well as you.

Josh's lips twitched slightly as he turned to open her gift to him. They twitched even more when he saw the framed photograph of herself. "I should have known what kind of gifts a photographer gives," he teased her. "It's beautiful. Almost as beautiful as the real thing."

His kiss was neither light nor quick and, although his arms did not touch her, Tracy could not have moved to save her life. His lips and the spell they cast imprisoned her just as tightly as his embrace would have.

"Are you sure you two don't want some privacy?" Dan teased them. "We can all go and have breakfast and leave you alone."

Tracy blushed, much to everyone's amusement, and pulled away. She felt confused and wished desperately that she could have some time to herself. Why was he acting this way after all the things he had said last night? She knew the reason behind her own behavior: she was attracted to him. She liked the feel of his arms around her and the touch of his lips on hers. But what about him? Was this all part of the masquerade? What else could it be, when he knew about David and the reasons her marriage had failed?

The children had a few small presents to open and, by the time they were done, Monica and her family had arrived. Mrs. Rettinger was busy making breakfast for them all. To escape Josh for a time, Tracy offered to help Joan set the table.

Since there were so many people, the children would eat in the kitchen and the adults in the dining room. The food would be served buffet-style on the kitchen counters. Once the places were set, Joan left Tracy pouring glasses of orange juice at the dining table, while she filled the cream pitchers and sugar bowls in the kitchen.

"I haven't had a real chance to wish you a merry Christmas," a soft voice behind Tracy said.

She turned around slowly, reluctant to encounter Monica on her own. For some reason, she mistrusted this soft-spoken, seemingly gentle woman.

"Hello, Monica. Merry Christmas," she forced herself to say.

"I saw the picture you gave Aunt Clara and Uncle John," Monica said quietly. "It certainly pleased them."

"I'm so glad." Tracy was not about to gush and simper or pretend to enjoy Monica's company. "I hoped that it would." She glanced toward the door, wishing that Josh would appear to rescue her, but the doorway remained empty.

"We were all so pleased to meet you," Monica went on. "I'm afraid that we had given up hope that Josh would ever marry again. We had been so happy together that—" She stopped suddenly with a frown. "Why are you wearing my cameo?" she asked, her voice harsh.

Tracy's hand went automatically up to the brooch at her throat. "Your cameo?" she said bravely, although a tremor of fear ran through her. "Josh gave it to me."

"He gave it to you?" Monica hissed. "He gave it to *me*. On our wedding day. It was his grandmother's and he had been very close to her. I found it was missing after our divorce, but I never dreamed that he had taken it back."

"Why not?" Tracy shrugged, hoping to appear unconcerned. "It belonged in his family. He had a right to keep it, and to give it to someone else if he chose."

Monica was annoyed that Tracy seemed so calm. "I suppose it is cheaper this way," she said in a too-sweet voice. "And if it doesn't bother you that you're getting everything secondhand, including him, it certainly doesn't bother me. I know he'll never love you the way he loved me." With a haughty sniff, Monica turned and left the room.

Tracy stared after her for a moment, then continued to pour the small glasses of orange juice, although her hands were shaking. Monica had intended to upset her and she had. Not with her rude little insinuations, which were almost laughable, but because of the realization that the brooch was special. It meant something to Josh, and by giving it to her, or pretending to give it to her, it became another part of their act. It was something that would be returned when they got back to Chicago.

For a few minutes, she had let herself dream that he gave it to her because he wanted her to have it. It had been a foolish delusion, she knew, because she was so vulnerable. Her heart had built castles in just a few moments and even though Monica's words had torn them down, Tracy feared the ruins would never disappear completely. The memory of these few days with Josh were going to be painful for a long time to come, because she had been stupid enough to forget he was acting a part, and had let her heart reach out toward him.

Chapter Five

WHEN TRACY WENT OFF to help prepare breakfast, Josh frowned. He had hoped to have some time alone with her to undo the damage that he had done the night before with his stupid declaration of independence. He had only been trying to be fair to both of them. How was he to know that she would turn out to be very different from what he'd thought? But she had been gone before he had a chance to ask her if she'd like to take Paddy for a walk. Damnit, he had the feeling he was going to have to make an appointment if he wanted to talk to her by herself.

He got a garbage bag and began to pick up the discarded wrapping paper, while Dan and Charlie helped the two boys put their train together. That was the problem with these family get-togethers. There were too damn many people, all expecting you to be cheerful and friendly, when the only thing you wanted to do was get to know one particular person better.

"I've got to hand it to you," Josh's father said, coming over to help pick up. "You've really picked a winner this time. Your Tracy is one special lady."

Josh nodded, grateful that someone had shredded up some paper and that it required his concentration to pick up all the little pieces. It was somewhat galling to realize that that "winner" had not been his choice at all. He had picked Denise, who would have made her boredom very plain and probably spoiled the holiday for everyone. If she had brought a gift at all, it probably would have been one of those huge books of photographs that collect dust on coffee tables, or a box of liqueured chocolates.

No, Tracy was the right one to bring here. They all loved her, and she got along with his family better than he did. Everything was working out beautifully. Why then couldn't he just relax and enjoy it? Why did it bother him so that Tracy lumped him in the same category as her stray dogs and cats?

By the time breakfast was ready, Josh had decided that he was just overreacting to Tracy's sensitivity. She had given his parents a truly thoughtful gift, and since the whole purpose of this masquerade had been to put their minds at ease, naturally he was pleased that it was succeeding so well. Of course, she was an attractive young woman and he was not exactly elderly. It was only normal that he should find her presence exciting and his own interest stirring. Once they got back to Chicago, though, he knew that things would fall back into perspective. She would go back to her cats and dogs and he would find a replacement for Denise.

Quite pleased with his reasoning, Josh filled his plate with eggs, sausage, and warm bread. He had regained his equilibrium and happily chatted with Charlie, who was waiting with him for some more pancakes to be cooked. Once his plate was filled to overflowing, he went into the dining room, only to stop short at the discovery that all the seats near Tracy were filled.

"I see I'm not to be allowed to sit near my own fiancée," he grumbled as he went to the last empty chair. Everyone just laughed good-naturedly, but no one offered to give up a seat.

His appetite mysteriously diminished, Josh forced himself to eat some of his food. Monica was sitting across from him and chattering constantly, to his great annoyance, so he could not hear what Tracy was saying. She didn't seem to be eating anything, though, and he frowned at her, wondering if something was wrong.

"Tracy's pictures were very nice." Monica's gushings attracted his attention. "I never could take a decent picture even with one of those instant cameras." She giggled, inviting the others to appreciate her incompetence.

"I always thought it was the other end of the camera that you were interested in," Josh snapped. He didn't know what Monica was getting at, but she had better leave Tracy alone.

"Oh, Josh," Monica giggled again, loudly enough for the whole table to hear. "Trust you to remember how many pictures you always wanted of me."

It was a downright lie, but hardly worth making a scene over. Josh glanced down at Tracy, wanting to reassure her, but she seemed absorbed in conversation with his father. Not that she would care if I had a million pictures of Monica, he reminded himself. He went back to picking at his food.

"Actually, when I saw those pictures, I was thinking of Tom and Sandy," Monica went on in her breathless voice. "They're getting married in a couple of weeks, and Tracy could take the pictures."

Josh raised his head to glare at her. "She doesn't do weddings," he informed her.

Monica was not at all embarrassed and turned her pleading little look toward Tracy. "They're such special friends," she simpered. "Almost a part of the family."

Tracy looked rather uneasy, as if she felt hemmed in and not certain how to refuse. "I really don't have the experience . . . ," she began.

"Oh, what experience do you need to take a few snapshots?" Monica scoffed her worries away. "It's three weeks from Saturday, the ceremony's at three and the reception is right afterward."

"I don't really think—" Tracy tried again.

"Nonsense, darling," Josh interrupted her smoothly with a gentle smile. Monica was just not that easy to get rid of. "Of course you'd be happy to do it." He turned away from Tracy's stunned face to look at Monica. "She charges a flat fee of five hundred for three hours' work and a maximum of one hundred shots. All reprints and enlargements are extra, of course. If you give her Sandy's address, she can send her a contract."

Monica just stared at him for a moment, shocked speechless. "You shouldn't kid so," she said after a moment, with a slightly hesitant laugh.

Josh picked up a piece of bread and nonchalantly buttered it. "Who's kidding?" he shrugged. "She's an award-winning photographer. Sandy'd be damn lucky to get her at that price." He ventured a glance down at Tracy, and saw the gleam of laughter in her eye. Uh-oh, he'd pay for that remark for sure. He'd be reminded of it every time she was assigned to him.

Monica did not pursue the subject, turning instead to Joan to begin some involved conversation, so Josh knew that he had won. He looked down the table toward Tracy, wanting to share the humor in the situation with her, but her attention had already been claimed by Dan.

As soon as breakfast was over, Josh decided not to take any more chances and announced that he and Tracy were going out for a while. "I've promised to show her the high spots of Harvard," he explained to everyone when he saw her questioning look. Before she could protest, he had her arm and was leading her toward the front door.

"That was really rude," she informed him as he held her coat out for her. "I should be staying to help clean up."

"There's enough people here to wash all the dishes in the house in an hour," Josh noted. He put his own coat on, then stopped. "Why don't you bring your camera?" he suggested.

Tracy gave him a suspicious glance, but hurried up the stairs to get the camera. A few minutes later, they were in Josh's car, pulling away from his parents' house.

They rode in silence for a short while. Now that he had her alone, Josh was trying to decide on his next move. All that nonsense he had said last night about her not being his type was just that—nonsense. The trouble was, just how could he undo the damage he had already done? Maybe if he found something really interesting for her to photograph, she would—

"Why are you always running away from Monica?" Tracy asked suddenly.

Josh glanced at her quickly in astonishment. "What the hell are you talking about?"

"It's obvious that you're still in love with her," she went on. "Your family may be fooled about your feelings because of our supposed engagement, but I'm not."

She spoke with such confidence that Josh did not know whether to laugh or explode with rage. He pulled the car off to the side of the road and turned to face her, his left hand resting on the dashboard.

"I am not in love with Monica," he said most emphatically. "And I am not running away. I thought you might need a break from her."

"Me?" Tracy looked so nonplussed that some of Josh's anger faded.

"Well, you're the one she zeros in on," he pointed out. "And it wasn't just that nonsense about the pictures. From the way you were acting at breakfast, I was sure she had done something else."

He was certain that he had hit close to home, for Tracy turned to stare out the window. "Actually, we did have a little talk," she admitted and turned back to smile at him. "Only I wasn't quite as shocked and devastated as she had hoped."

Josh frowned. He might have known Monica would be up to no good. "What was it about?"

"How you stole the cameo from her," Tracy told him with a laugh. "It was terribly precious to her and she never, never would have let it go. Apparently, though, *you* were expendable," she added.

"It doesn't sound like it bothered you to receive stolen merchandise," he said lightly, although he was rather puzzled. She seemed to be taking Monica's interference as a joke now; yet at breakfast she could hardly eat.

"Well, she did rather spoil the whole effect by telling me that it had been your grandmother's," Tracy said. "So I didn't think she had any right to keep it once you were divorced."

"If it didn't bother you, why couldn't you eat?" he persisted.

Tracy's rather determined cheerfulness slipped slightly. "Breakfast isn't my favorite meal," she said with a shrug. "I rarely eat much."

"Oh?"

She frowned at his obvious disbelief. "All right, so she got me mad," she admitted heatedly. "What's so important about that?"

"What else did she say?" he demanded.

Tracy sighed and leaned back in her seat. Her eyes stared straight ahead of her, out the front window. "Nothing really," she told him. "It was just her attitude. I'm afraid I don't like your Monica very much."

Josh laughed at her reluctance to admit it. "I don't either," he said with a warm smile.

Tracy was astonished at his admission, and didn't bother to hide it. "But you were married to her!" she exclaimed.

Josh shrugged and pulled the car back on the road. "And it was a mistake from the words 'I do.' Not exactly a match made in heaven."

Tracy did not like to admit that the feeling of exultation racing through her was from the knowledge that he was not in love with Monica; but it was true. She felt like jumping up and down or singing or, she thought with a sly glance at him, like kissing him.

"How'd you happen to marry her if you weren't in love?" she asked curiously. She was watching out the window as they turned toward downtown Harvard, pretending only mild interest in the question.

"I was never quite sure," he said with a laugh, then sobered up slightly. "Actually, she was the girl that half the town was in love with. Or at least the entire male half of my generation. She was absolutely gorgeous fifteen years and thirty pounds ago."

Tracy smiled secretly, the twice-weekly aerobic classes suddenly worthwhile.

Josh went on. "She was a cheerleader, homecoming queen, and the Milk Queen in Harvard's milk festival. Everybody wanted a chance with her, but by the time she graduated from high school and was working part-time at the bank, she had become bored with the local male population. I had graduated from Northwestern and landed a job out west with a paper in L.A. I started to make a name for myself and when the Chicago *Daily News* offered me a job, I took it. I was able to come home pretty frequently and, on one of those visits, I met Monica."

He paused for a moment to negotiate a turn. "I still remember how beautiful she looked that day. She was all in pink and looked like a flower. Her car had stalled down the street from our house and she had come to use the phone."

"And you just happened to be home," Tracy said dryly. "My, my, what a coincidence!"

Josh laughed out loud. "Yes, well, I wasn't quite so wise back then. All I saw was this luscious

young lady who was terribly in awe of my presti-
gious position."

"So naturally you married her. Then what happened?"

"Well, Chicago was not quite like Harvard. No
one cared that she had been Milk Queen, but I was
not about to move back and work for the Harvard
Herald as she wanted. Things just kept getting
worse until we called it quits. She scurried back
to Harvard and married Charlie, who had had
the good sense to become a vice-president at the
bank."

"You make it sound as if she chose him for his
position." Tracy frowned.

"Hey, let's face it," Josh pointed out. "She
wasn't going to marry anybody who couldn't give
her the social position she thought she deserved.
She may be fond of Charlie, but the only one she
really loves is herself."

"What a waste!" Tracy sighed.

"The waste is in spending time talking about
her," Josh noted as he turned onto Ayer Street.
Downtown Harvard was deserted and he pulled
into a parking place in front of the Masonic Lodge.
"I can think of any number of more interesting
ways to spend my time."

His hazel eyes carried a sensual message that
was impossible to ignore. They looked deep into
hers, trying to judge her emotions and response.
Tracy gazed back at him confidently; the feelings
that he aroused were too primitive and too strong
for her to pretend coyness.

Deep inside her she marveled that, although he
knew the truth about her, he had not backed away.
A delicious shiver of anticipation raced through

her. His family was not in sight and there was no one around for him to be trying to impress. Could it be that he felt that same magnetic attraction that she kept experiencing? That same tingling excitement whenever they were together?

Josh came around to her side of the car to help her out. Even through her bulky down jacket, she was startlingly aware of his touch on her arm. It caused her blood to race as she imagined quite vividly the touch of his hands on her body. The longings that shook her were unbelievably strong and they fought with the instinctive wariness that was David's legacy.

Some of Tracy's desires must have glimmered in her eyes, for Josh did not move away from her after he closed her door. He gazed deep into her eyes for a long moment, drinking in the passion that was awakening there. Then, slowly, he bent his head so that his lips touched hers in the gentlest of caresses. It was a whisper, a teasing touch that wasn't the slightest bit satisfying to Tracy.

His hands slid across her back. They did not pull her closer, but held her prisoner as his lips began their next descent. Still moving with agonizing slowness, they exerted the barest of pressure against her lips, tantalizing her again and again, until she thought she would die of longing.

Just as her body seemed to melt and sway toward him, his arms tightened their hold and drew her to him. Locked in his iron embrace, her lips reached up gladly for his. The gentle teasing was gone as his mouth assaulted hers, his touch rough and hungry. She felt as if her whole body were being crushed by his lips and the ever-tightening hold of his arms, but the sensation served only to heighten her desire.

Her own arms were around his body, her fingers frustrated by the gloves that encased them as they longed to feel his muscles move beneath his skin. She needed his body close to hers, but the bulkiness of the winter coats let only their lips merge.

Echoing her needs, Josh's tongue slipped into the waiting warmth of her mouth. Powerfully, it explored the hidden recesses, tasting of her sweetness and surging with sexual desire.

Suddenly Josh stepped back, his arms holding her body away from his, his breathing rapid. Tracy felt a sudden pang of loneliness and desertion as she gazed up into his eyes, still darkened with passion.

"I think you'd better take some pictures," he said, his voice hoarse and unsteady. "This isn't quite the setting for what I'd like to do."

Tracy smiled up at him. The ache was still there, but she knew he was right. "Yeah, and the backseats of cars never were my style."

They walked across the street together, their bodies close but carefully not touching. Tracy tried to put his disturbing presence from her mind. Although she failed miserably, it was some consolation to know that she affected him as strongly as he affected her.

In a frantic attempt to appear in control of herself, Tracy looked around her. "How about if we start our tour with that?" she suggested, pointing to a large statue of a black-and-white cow that was on a pedestal in the middle of the street.

Josh picked up her light mood. "Harmilda

would be the perfect beginning." He took Tracy's hand and led her around the front of the statue, where she took a few pictures.

"Obviously, since it is preoccupied with milk, Harvard is essentially a dairy-farm area," Josh told her. "Or it was. The number of actual dairy farms has decreased in the last few years, but it still holds on to its Milk Festival." He looked beyond the statue down the deserted street. "On Milk Day, Ayer Street is whitewashed and becomes the Milky Way, and a parade goes down it. The queen takes her bath in milk down here by the statue and then presides over such excitements as milking contests, milk-drinking contests, and cattle shows."

"I thought it was fun the year I was here," Tracy pointed out.

Josh nodded somewhat reluctantly. "You only have to be here an hour and you know you're far from Chicago," he agreed: "Farther than the actual sixty-five miles."

He took her arm and they walked over to the sidewalk and then down the block. At first glance, the old two-story buildings all seemed very much the same, but they actually varied marvelously in the ornate cornices that went across their flat roofs. Most of them had three tall, narrow windows across the second floor with neat curtains and plants inside. There were no broken or boarded-up windows here.

Lined up perfectly, the buildings varied from yellow to red brick, while the simple storefront signs added more color. The only building that had succumbed to the modernization of cedar and dark brown brick was the Harvard Theatre, which also sported a "For Rent or Sale" sign.

"That's where I worked in the winters during high school," Josh said, pointing across the street to the Krause-Gabinski Hardware Store. "I became an expert on nail sizes."

"How valuable!" Tracy murmured as she gazed around her. For all she knew, they could have gone back in time, for the town seemed ageless. It was incredibly neat. Even the gas-station building was old, but its white-painted brick walls were spotless. "It must have been very nice growing up in a town like this."

Josh shrugged. "It had its disadvantages. Everybody knows everything about you," he pointed out. "So when you screw up, your mother knows before you even get home."

"And were you often in trouble?" she asked.

He looked surprised at her question. "Constantly," he admitted with a smile. "Although I wasn't really all that bad. It's just that Charlie and Dan were never caught and I was."

Tracy laughed, trying hard to imagine Josh as a teenager. He seemed so carefully controlled and reserved that she couldn't see him as carefree, the way young people should be. Had Monica done that to him?

As they rounded the corner by the Chamber of Commerce, a carillon at the First Presbyterian Church began to play Christmas carols. Tracy sighed. It was almost as if they were playing just for them.

"Something the matter?" Josh frowned.

She shook her head. "No, it's just a beautiful Christmas," she said, wondering if he would mock her sentimentality. But he didn't. Rather, he took her arm, and they walked back to the car in silence.

Andrea Edwards

After leaving the downtown area, they drove north a few blocks and then turned right. "That's Monica and Charlie's house," Josh said, slowing down to point out a gray Queen Anne house on their right.

Three stories high, the house was trimmed with ornately carved woodenwork that was painted an immaculate white, as were the porch posts and balusters. The windows were large and topped with a stained-glass panel. The house was beautiful in design, and it was obvious that its owners thought so too. Everything about it was perfectly kept up.

Tracy felt a tingling of jealousy as they pulled away. Her fingers itched to take pictures of it, but she knew a photograph would never satisfy her. That was the type of house she had always wanted to own. What fun it would be to decorate the odd-shaped rooms, and marvel at the craftsmanship that went into its building! It didn't seem fair that Monica should have something so beautiful.

"That's the kind of house that I had always wanted," she admitted to Josh.

"Oh? I guess there are some around Chicago," he said. "You should buy one and refurbish it."

Tracy shook her head, staring out the window. "They're all so battered and worn it wouldn't be the same. You could never match the stained-glass panels, assuming that any originals were even left. I guess it'll just stay a dream," she sighed.

"It's cheaper that way," he laughed. "Think how much they must pay for painting. Charlie sure doesn't climb around keeping that so perfect. In fact, he'd probably be satisfied with an apartment over Stafford's Shoes. It's Monica that wants the castle."

"Well, it's a beautiful castle," Tracy admitted as they pulled into the parking lot of a tiny park.

"I thought you'd want some nature shots," Josh explained when she gave him a puzzled look.

They were at the end of Brown Street, with the municipal swimming pool to their left and the park in front of them. A wire backstop marked a baseball field to their right.

"Is that the site of your great baseball career?" she asked.

"Definitely," Josh said wryly. "The strikeout champ of Harvard at age nine. I had to pack up my dreams of playing pro and choose a new career."

Tracy took a couple of shots of the deserted, snow-covered field. "Is that when you decided to become a writer?"

"No, I think my next choice was pirate. I thought it would be fun to have a wooden leg."

Tracy turned to stare at him, laughing at his sheepish look. "Well, I had just read *Treasure Island,*" he admitted. "And it seemed more exciting than being a farmer in Harvard all my life."

She just shook her head; she was laughing too hard to talk. Josh frowned at her when tears trickled down her cheeks. "You must have had crazy dreams, too," he muttered.

She nodded and forced herself to stop laughing. "Not that strange, though."

"Oh?"

They walked into the small park. The path was covered with snow, but Josh led her toward a small red bridge that went over a tiny creek.

"You have to understand that I grew up in awkward times for girls," Tracy warned him. "We started out dreaming of a house and family, but then learned we could actually have other things.''

''So what did you dream of?''

She took a picture of the creek, tiny but fast-moving, as it cut its way through the snow. ''For a while, I decided I was the kidnapped daughter of a gypsy king, and would soon be restored to my rightful parents. I spent a great deal of time getting ready for their return, but my mom drew the line at calling me Princess Tracy.''

''That's pretty dumb,'' Josh teased.

''Oh, I don't know,'' she argued. ''I can curtsy very well now.''

He laughed out loud and took her arm, holding it tightly to his side as he led her over the bridge and toward the swing sets. ''So when did you decide that the king was never coming for you?''

''I'm not sure I ever did,'' she admitted. ''I just sort of forgot about it and became highly idealistic. I was going to join the Peace Corps and save the world.''

Josh snickered and she frowned haughtily at him, hiding a smile. ''I'll have you know I was very serious about it. I even tried to sleep with my electric blanket turned off to harden myself to the rigors of the wild.''

Josh laughed even harder and she joined him. It felt so right to be silly and share little secrets, as if they belonged together. That led her thoughts in dangerous directions, though, and she turned slowly away from him. Better stick to the reason you came out here, she told herself. Don't build dreams on the basis of a few shared memories. Doesn't everyone get nostalgic around Christmas?

Determinedly, Tracy took a number of pictures.

The snow on the tree-covered hills, the deserted swing sets, the tiny creek that rushed under the red bridge, and the cows in the adjacent field. Birds feeding, and the delicate pattern of snow on the bark of the oak trees. Soon the pictures became an escape, for if she concentrated on them, she didn't have to think about Josh and his puzzling behavior.

As pleasant as the circle of his arms had been, she could not keep her old fears from coming back. After his cold behavior last night, why did he suddenly seem as if he couldn't get enough of her company? Was he really attracted to her? Or was he just bored being at home without Denise and looking for a part-time playmate?

She knew the attraction she felt toward him was not going to be satisfied with a substitute role, but why would he suddenly want her now when he had hated the sight of her for the past two years? The trouble was, she wanted him as much as he seemed to want her, and his reasons were totally unimportant. All that really bothered her was how long she was going to have to wait to get back in his arms again.

Chapter Six

"PADDY!" TRACY CALLED softly as she peered into the kitchen.

Mrs. Rettinger, Joan, and Monica were seated at the table, peeling the already cooked potatoes for potato salad for dinner. They were laughing and talking together, but Mrs. Rettinger looked up when Tracy poked her head in.

"I think he's with John, dear," she told Tracy. She turned back to the other women. "He didn't go with the children, did he?" There was a general murmur of agreement that her dog was about somewhere. "Why don't you check John's study?" Mrs. Rettinger suggested, going back to her peeling.

Tracy nodded and left the room. She and Josh had been out for several hours and she felt guilty about leaving Paddy at his parents'. Not that she could have taken him along, she realized. Paddy did not thrive on cold weather, and viewed birds, squirrels, and rabbits as dangerous varmints to be chased away before they viciously tore her body apart.

Even when they returned, Tracy had not been exactly worried about the needs of her dog. In fact, with the shock of discovering that she and Josh were suffering from the same curiously strong attraction to each other, Paddy was the farthest thing from her mind.

They had driven home in silence, Tracy preoccupied with her need for Josh and certain that his thoughts were likewise occupied. What were they going to do? As much as she would like to, they could hardly say hello to everyone, then slip up to his room for a few hours of passion. So, what would Josh suggest? A midnight assignation? It would have to be in his room, for the daybed she was sleeping on was hardly designed for a passionate tryst.

To her total astonishment, though, when they entered the house, Josh had said nothing to her, either by word or look. He just hung up their coats in silence and then sauntered into the living room to page through the set of books he had gotten from his parents. It was, Tracy marveled, as if those few hours of shared intimacy had never happened.

Her only consolation, she thought, was that she hadn't said anything to indicate her willingness to sleep with him. Her dogs and cats were definitely much safer. It was then that she remembered Paddy and went to the kitchen to look for him.

Mr. Rettinger's study was in the opposite corner of the house from the living room, so Tracy headed down the quiet hallway with relief. She wasn't up to facing Josh just yet.

"Paddy," she called again, then stopped suddenly, the stillness penetrating her mind. It was too deserted this way. Paddy liked to be around people. She was just about to turn around when a voice stopped her.

"He's in here," Mr. Rettinger called.

Tracy went to the door of the study and looked in. It was a small room, paneled in a warm, light brown with bookshelves and trophy cases lining the walls. In one corner was a beat-up-looking desk, and in the center of the room a sofa and two chairs. Mr. Rettinger was reclining on the sofa, his feet up on a small table. Paddy was lying next to him, his furry head resting in the man's lap. The wagging of her dog's tail was the only sign that he was aware of her presence.

"I think you're spoiling him," Tracy laughed. "He's going to demand such treatment at home."

Mr. Rettinger did not laugh, but sadly patted Paddy's head. "He's just taking pity on a useless old man," he sighed. "I'm sure he'd rather be out skating with the kids."

Tracy was surprised at the dejection in his voice and wondered what had happened to cause it. She walked over to a chair and sat down. "I can assure you that Paddy would not like to be outside," she told him with a smile. "He feels the cold too much. I'd say he's the useless old man, not you."

Josh's father shook his head. "No, but it's sweet of you to say so," he said quietly. "You're a nice person. I can see why Josh loves you so."

She was not certain what kind of response to make, so she just laughed. "Is it so obvious then?"

"As obvious as your love for him," Mr. Rettinger insisted. Tracy smiled slightly, unnerved by the realization that her expressions were being interpreted. "You two look at each other like no one else exists. It must be nice to be young and in love," he sighed.

Tracy was not certain just what her feelings for Josh were, but she knew she was not in love with him. Love just didn't descend on you that way—not in real life. This was a fleeting attraction or proximity, or just a healthy case of lust, but it certainly wasn't love. It couldn't be, could it?

She stood up to escape her disturbing thoughts and wandered over to one of the trophy cases in which ribbons from county and state fairs were displayed. Canning, gardening, quilting, and livestock awards were all represented, along with pictures of the awarding of the prize. Could that really be Josh as a scrawny twelve-year-old, his arm proudly around the neck of a calf?

"Why do Monica and Charlie spend so much time here?" Tracy asked suddenly, turning around. "It seems strange after she and Josh were divorced."

"It was awkward for a time," Mr. Rettinger admitted. "But Charlie's mother had died when he was six, and he had spent a lot of time around here after that. Almost like another son. When he and Monica wanted to marry we had to decide if we wanted to exclude Charlie or try to accept her."

"But weren't you taking a chance of driving Josh away?"

He shrugged. "We knew that Josh would understand, and we figured that he could handle a bitch like Monica."

Tracy stared at him in surprise and walked slowly back toward her chair.

"Oh, come now," he laughed at the shocked expression on her face. "You can't tell me that you thought she was a wonderful person. Josh should never have married her and we both know it."

"Well, I could see that," she admitted reluctantly. "But I wasn't sure anyone else agreed. She doesn't appear to be the giving type."

"Nope, that she isn't," he agreed. "Not that Josh would do all the taking. You'll see after you're married. He can be the most generous person around. But there'll be times when he needs to have a totally unselfish person. Someone who'll give him everything and more."

"It's like that in any marriage," Tracy pointed out, shaken by the intimate picture of life with Josh that had jumped into her mind.

Mr. Rettinger nodded. "In any good marriage," he corrected her, leaning forward with an air of confidentiality. "But it wasn't like that in Josh and Monica's. That's what you're going to have to remember. It's going to take him time to trust you. He was hurt badly before and you have to give him time."

Tracy did not like the desire that leapt through her blood. It wasn't the physical desire that she had discovered in Josh's arms, but an emotional desire to guard him, to keep him safe while she found the same security with him. She could be patient and help him learn to love again.

Standing up abruptly, Tracy desperately sought a way to stop her train of thoughts. "You people have certainly made me feel like a part of the family," she said quickly. "Not just me, but my mangy old mutt, too." She made a face at Paddy, who was still too comfortable to move.

"Hey, he's not just some old mutt," Mr. Rettinger protested with a laugh.

"True, and he isn't even mine."

Mr. Rettinger frowned. "He isn't?"

"No," Tracy said, explaining about the animal

shelter. "As much as I love him, my life isn't settled enough for a sick dog. I'm on a different schedule every day and it's hard to feed him at the right times." She looked up suddenly, an idea flashing in her eyes. "Hey, how'd you like a dog?"

"You're serious?"

"Sure," she said eagerly, sitting down again. "Of course, he's a responsibility. He'll be totally dependent on you for his insulin shots, his meals, everything. Much more than a regular dog," she warned him.

"I know that," he scoffed. "But it hardly counts when you're talking about a friend."

Tracy could not keep from smiling. "Are you sure you're not too old for the job?"

"I'm too old for that kind of disrespect, young lady," he laughed and stood up. He held out his arm to her. "Let's go tell Clara the good news."

"What do you mean, you're leaving tonight?" Mrs. Rettinger stopped pouring the coffee and stared at Josh. "You said you were staying until lunchtime tomorrow."

"I know what we had planned." Josh put down his napkin and leaned back from the table. "But there's a winter storm warning out for tonight. If we don't get back to town tonight, we might not make it for a couple of days."

"We wouldn't mind," his father said.

Josh smiled at him. "Unfortunately, our bosses might. We've both got to get back to work." He glanced at his watch. "I thought if we left by eight, we'd be home by ten or eleven and still miss the storm by a few hours."

Mrs. Rettinger went back to pouring the coffee

while Tracy and Joan were cleaning the dirty dinner dishes from the table. "We get winter storm warnings every week," she pointed out. "Most of them never even amount to an inch of snow. Why are you taking this one so seriously?"

"Because this storm has already dumped a foot and a half of snow in Nebraska and Iowa," Josh told her. "And they're predicting that much for northern Illinois."

Monica carried in a chocolate whipped-cream cake that was rolled up and iced to look like a Yule log, while Tracy brought in two plates of Christmas cookies and placed them at either end of the table. Mrs. Rettinger turned to her as she took her seat next to Josh.

"Can't you persuade him to stay longer?" she pleaded with Tracy.

Smiling gently, Tracy shook her head. "As much as I'd love to stay an extra day, I'm afraid Josh is right. We really ought to get back before the storm." The older woman looked disappointed, but Tracy turned her attention to the cake that Monica was slicing. This whole masquerade was ridiculous, and the sooner it was over, the happier she'd be. She was letting herself get involved with Josh, and that was not only stupid, it was downright dangerous.

For the rest of the dinner and the few hours afterward, Mrs. Rettinger tried to persuade them to stay until the next day, but Josh was firm. By eight o'clock he had his and Tracy's suitcases packed into the car, along with the tins of cookies that his mother had prepared and two six-packs of Point beer that his father had gotten him from Wisconsin. The good-byes were said all around and by 8:05 he and Tracy were on their way.

They rode in silence until Harvard was left behind them. Tracy spent the time staring out the window, although it was too dark to see anything but an occasional lighted house set back from the road. It hardly mattered, since her mind was far away, reliving those few times, scattered over the past two days, when she had felt really close to Josh.

She remembered more than the delirious moments in his arms, although those came back vividly, leaving an aching loneliness in their wake. There had been occasions when they were really talking, when one had reached out to the other with understanding and concern. Would all that be forgotten now that they had left Harvard?

Who are you trying to kid? she asked herself angrily. He had made it very clear that first night that there never would be anything between them. In spite of his erratic behavior, she knew nothing had changed.

"I hope you didn't mind leaving early," Josh said. His voice sounded loud in the stillness and Tracy started slightly.

"No, of course not," she assured him. Then some demon inside her forced her to add, "It was hard enough to keep up the masquerade for the two days we were there. If we had been stranded by the snow, I'm sure I would have given everything away." It was all a lie, she knew, since she had constantly forgotten that she was playing a part, but it soothed her ego to hear the words spoken out loud.

"True, it would have been hard," Josh muttered absently as he passed another car.

Tracy lapsed once more into her dreamlike state, wishing he would have denied her words, yet knowing that he never would. Damn! She had been one prize fool ever to agree to the whole stupid arrangement.

"Damn!"

Tracy turned in surprise to find Josh echoing her thoughts.

"I thought we'd miss the storm, leaving when we did," he said.

She turned to look out the window and saw, with surprise, that it was snowing. Not just flurries, either, but large heavy flakes that seemed to be coming down rapidly. A quick glance at her watch told her that they had left his parents' only a half hour earlier. They were barely past Woodstock. "Do you think we ought to go back?"

He didn't answer for a moment, peering ahead into the swirling snow that his headlights illuminated. "No," he said finally. "We'd be heading into it. If we keep moving, maybe we can beat the damn thing."

Since Josh did not ask for her opinion, Tracy said nothing but kept watching out the windows. No reassuring house lights were visible any longer. The snow danced in a frenzy around the car until Tracy could not be certain they were even moving in the right direction.

For the next hour the storm got progressively worse. Occasionally another car would join them for a short passage on the highway, but would soon turn off and disappear into the darkness, leaving them alone again. The few farmhouses that were close enough to the road to be visible beckoned as havens of warmth and security, a vague longing for their comfort lingering long after their lights had disappeared. Tracy said nothing as they struggled forward, but her hands were clenched together nervously as she willed the car up each icy hill.

A flashing orange light off to one side showed a state police car helping a motorist who had skidded into a ditch. They passed it in silence, the orange light a somber warning that hung heavily in the air.

The wind picked up and each curve and hill became their enemy in the battle to keep the car on the road. The blast of wind would slow their progress while the blinding snow dared them to guess in which direction safety lay.

At one curve, the wind had blown the snow from the pavement and in doing so, polished the glaze of ice to a deadly sheen. When Josh's car hit it, the wheels slipped from his control, and he made a desperate attempt to steer. The wind and snow just mocked his efforts, though, as the car spun around wildly, skidding across the center line. As Tracy's heart climbed into her mouth, the lights of an oncoming truck suddenly came bearing down on them with deadly aim. With one final lurch, the car stopped at the side of the road, and the truck was able to veer around them.

Slowly, Tracy let out her breath and leaned back against the seat, shaking with cold and fright.

"Are you all right?" Josh asked. His voice was none too steady, and Tracy turned to nod at him.

"Yeah," she whispered, realizing that he couldn't see her nod. "Just a little shaky."

Josh started the car and carefully pulled back

onto their own side of the road. "I think there's a place ahead where we'd better stop for the night," he said. "Next time we might not be so lucky."

Tracy peered out the window, but the lights that had been so comforting seemed to have deserted them. "Wouldn't you know that there'd be nothing now?" she muttered in frustration after peering into the darkness for what seemed like hours.

"It's not much farther, don't worry," he said. His voice was soothing and the hand that reached over to hold hers had a comforting strength to it. She relaxed slightly and continued to look.

After another ten minutes, lights appeared off to their right. "Something's coming," Tracy warned him as the Black Forest Motel suddenly loomed at the side of the road.

Josh pulled quickly off the road and onto a snow-filled driveway, stopping before a small green building with a neon "Office" sign above the door.

"Let's hope they've still got room," he said and hurried out of the car and into the building.

Tracy shivered in the darkness, and looked over at the clock on the dashboard. It was only a little past ten. That nightmare ride had seemed to go on forever.

She looked nervously at the closed office door, the solitude of the car more frightening than the treacherous road. There was safety and strength in Josh's presence that she had not recognized until he left. Luckily, he was not gone more than a few minutes. His smile and the dangling key he held were proof of his success.

"Their last cabin," he said proudly. "Complete with heater and running water."

The prospect of actually being warm again occupied Tracy's mind as Josh inched the car around the corner of the office and past several other tiny little cabins before parking in front of the last one.

"Well, this one's it," Josh said, handing Tracy the key. "Why don't you open it up while I grab the bags?"

She nodded, taking the shopping bag of food that Mrs. Rettinger had fixed for them and leaving the suitcases for Josh. Running quickly through the snow, she opened the door easily and made it through just before Josh came rushing in.

"A real Taj Mahal," Josh laughed as he put down the cases and gazed about. Tracy just shrugged. She had found the heater and turned it on, the rumblings in the pipes an optimistic sign that warmth might not be far away.

Only after the rumblings had become regular did Tracy look around her to discover that the room was unbelievably small. The door was set near the corner of the cabin and opened into a tiny foyer that doubled as a closet, with a suitcase rack and wire hangers. Across from where they stood was the bathroom, resplendent in faded blue swans.

To their left was the rest of the cabin, most of the space taken up by the double bed that looked huge only because it filled up the tiny room. The turquoise corded cotton bedspread matched the stuffed vinyl headboard, but not the red plaid drapes or the gold rug.

"Well, the heat seems to work," Tracy laughed as she held her hands over the heating duct and felt the warmth coming out. "So I think I can live with the lovely decor."

Josh hung his coat up. "I'm sure they'd let you photograph it, if you want to copy their color scheme," he laughed. Spotting a phone on one of the small blond shelves that was supposed to pass for a nightstand, he went over to it. "I'd better call the folks and let them know we're okay. With the storm, they'll be up all night worrying."

Tracy nodded and went over to hang up her own coat, grateful for the time to think while Josh's attention was elsewhere. She knew that they had had no choice except to stop for the night, but this place did pose some problems with its one bed. There wasn't even enough floor space if one of them should opt for separate sleeping facilities.

Tracy watched as Josh laughed into the phone, her eyes going slowly over his broad back, her mind caressing his firm muscles. No, she thought, as she turned away suddenly. The problem was with her, not the motel room. She was the one that let her imagination run wild, letting herself build dreams that had no basis in reality.

Josh was certainly not bothered by the close confines in which they would be spending the night. But then he had not been bothered by her presence at any time, except for those few moments earlier today, and he had not let them bother him long.

Well, she could play it as cool and casual as he was. So what if there was no place else to sit but on the bed? It was childish to make a big production of it. She would follow his lead and not even try to analyze her own preferences for the night.

To show just how unaffected she was by his

presence, Tracy took off her boots, found a can of cookies, and sat down on the bed with them. Not just the edge of the bed, either, but comfortably in from the side.

"That looks like the right idea," Josh said as he hung up the phone and saw her eating. "This place doesn't run to a coffee shop and I think the one a half mile down the road is a bit out of our reach."

Tracy envied his relaxed manner as he sauntered across the small room to leave his boots by the door. How could he be so cool and casual when she was achingly conscious of his every move?

"Will you trade me some cookies for a beer?" he asked with a laugh, pulling a six-pack from the bag she had brought in.

"Sure," she said, trying to copy his free-and-easy tone, but fearing she fell a little short. "Although we probably should save some for breakfast."

He appeared not to notice the tension in her voice as he took two dark blue cans from the cardboard case and carried them over to the bed. "Beer and cookies for breakfast sounds almost as bad as cold pizza. I'm sure my stomach will protest."

After opening her can, he handed it to her, his fingers lightly brushing hers. The touch was gentle and purely accidental, Tracy knew, but it seemed to burn like fire and she could not help jerking her hand away. Then, of course, she felt like a fool.

"Hey, relax," Josh said quietly, no trace of mockery in his voice. "I'm not going to pounce on you."

Tracy tried to laugh. "I know that. It's just the storm. Made me a little jumpy." She took a long

114

drink of her beer and held out the cookies. "Better hurry up and get some. I tend to eat nonstop when I'm nervous."

Apparently he bought her excuse, for he sat down next to her, reclining on his side as he reached over for a handful of cookies. "Is this the can Mother gave you or mine?" he asked suspiciously as he pulled out two cookies covered with nuts.

Tracy held up the cover of the box, where a piece of tape with her name on it had been left. "Mine," she pointed out. "So be nice or I won't give you any more."

Josh took another nut-covered cookie. "I figured it had to be yours," he muttered with disgust. "There were too many of the good ones for it to be mine. She always says I'll eat anything, so why waste the good stuff on me."

Laughing, Tracy grabbed the next nut-covered cookie that he was reaching for. "Well, I can't say much about your appetite," she said after another drink of beer. "But I'll agree that your taste is not too discriminating."

Josh frowned at her and took a tiny pastry tart filled with pecans. "And what have I done to be so condemned?" he asked.

Tracy took another drink of her beer and was surprised that the can seemed so light. "Just look at Monica," she said, shaking the can near her ear. It sounded almost empty.

"I'd rather not, thank you," Josh replied sourly. He took another nut cup.

"Well, how about Denise?" Tracy suggested as she peered into the can. It looked almost empty.

"Cans are usually empty when you drink all the contents," Josh noted with a laugh.

Tracy frowned at him. "I didn't drink all this."

"Sure you did," he laughed again. "You've been guzzling it ever since I gave it to you." Tracy frowned even more severely but it did not seem to intimidate him at all. "Want another one?"

"I don't think I should," Tracy said haughtily.

Josh just smiled as he got up and took another can out of the bag. "It'll be good for you," he told her. "Help you to relax."

"I don't need help in relaxing," she informed him as she pulled a pillow out from under the bedspread. After putting it up against the headboard, she leaned back, stretching her slim legs out before her. "I know I am perfectly safe here with you. You've told me a million times," she added as her eyelids slipped down.

"I only remember mentioning it once," Josh said.

She heard the frown in his voice and opened her eyes. "Oh, you're always saying it," she laughed. "Let's see, I'm not your type. You're not that desperate. I'm unsophisticated and immature. And oh, yes, you prefer those books that you got for Christmas to me."

Josh just stared at her. "What are you talking about?"

Tracy looked about the room and then took her pullover sweater off, tossing it onto the foot of the bed. "It's getting hot in here, isn't it?"

A trace of a smile lurked in his eyes but she didn't see it. "It's been hot in here for a while but you haven't noticed."

She blinked at him in confusion, then looked

away to pick up a cookie, deciding to ignore his confusing remarks. "I was only quoting you," she told him. "Explaining how I know that I'm perfectly safe here with you." She took the can of beer that he was still holding in his hand and sipped at it before leaning back against the pillow again. She was pleased that she was handling this all so well.

"I'm confused," Josh admitted, looking up at her. His hazel eyes were a little too intense, so she bent over to search through the cookies. "I vaguely remember some of those remarks, although you've taken them a bit out of context. But that one about the books really stumps me. I can't believe I actually said that."

"Well, maybe not in words," she shrugged and bit into a gooey chocolate cookie. "But you sure were in a hurry to get to them when we got back from the park today."

Josh's smile of sudden understanding made her slightly uneasy, but she did not look away. "You know," he said lightly, "nothing cools a man's ardor faster than his mother's voice, unless it's the knowledge that his bedroom, to which he had the definite urge to whisk a certain young lady, was right above the kitchen where his mother, sister-in-law, and ex-wife were all sitting."

"Oh." Her voice was quiet.

"Yes, oh. And all those other remarks were the result of a guilty conscience," he went on. "Having discovered what a soft touch you were, it would have been all too easy to take advantage of you in any number of ways."

Tracy frowned at him. "And don't you think I might have objected?"

"No," he said honestly, picking out another

cookie. ''I think I could have had you believing anything I wanted you to believe.''

Tracy could not believe her ears! ''Boy! You've got some colossal ego!'' she cried, jumping up from the bed. ''I'm not a naive fool who can't tell when some man is on the make. You may think I'm wide-eyed and immature but underneath I'm pretty damn suspicious.''

''Oh, come on Tracy, don't get mad,'' he teased. ''You have to admit that you were softening.''

''I was not,'' she denied hotly. ''I thought you were an arrogant bastard and I still do.''

''At least give me some credit for the small bit of conscience you awoke,'' he snapped, rising to his feet as his patience wore thin. ''It was damned irritating.''

''It must be quite a relief that the whole farce is over with then,'' she said coldly, her stance rigid and unbending. ''You can return to Chicago and forget all about me unless we have the misfortune to be assigned to the same story.''

''I imagine that we can prevent that,'' he pointed out. ''Now if you don't mind, I'm going to get some sleep. I just pray that we can get out of here in the morning.''

''I'll bet,'' she sneered. ''Too bad your plan for tonight didn't work.''

He had started to rummage through his suitcase, but stopped to glare at her. ''What plan?''

''You didn't really think I fell for that 'last cabin' bit, did you? I mean, that was pretty transparent.''

''If you're so sure that they have more room, you're welcome to move to another cabin,'' he offered, an angry frown creasing his forehead. "Just walk over to the office and see what they say."

"A gentleman would not make me move," she snapped.

"So, who's a gentleman?" he shrugged. "But, in case you decide to stay, I plan to sleep in my clothes. That way I won't be accused of having nefarious schemes on your body while I'm asleep."

While Tracy continued to glare at him, he pulled out his toothbrush and toothpaste from his suitcase. Then, ignoring her, he went into the bathroom.

Once the door closed, Tracy walked across the room slowly. Her own toiletries were packed in one of the bags that Josh's parents had given her and the sight of it made her feel guilty for yelling at him. Of course, she knew this was the last cabin. And she had been softening. Melting was more like it. Just a look from him and she was ready to leap into his arms. Just because he had shown more responsibility than she would have was no reason to be angry at him.

All of her logic disappeared, though, when Josh came back out of the bathroom and gave her a black look. Hell, he was an arrogant bastard, she thought as she stormed into the bathroom, and she hated him.

"Tracy?"

The voice was barely a whisper and she ignored it, burrowing down deeper under the blanket. A feathery light touch tickled the side of her neck and she squirmed slightly. Must be one of the cats, she thought. "Go 'way," she muttered, wanting to go back to sleep.

"Am I really an arrogant bastard?"

Definitely not one of the cats, she realized as she woke up with a shock. How long had she been asleep? It felt like the middle of the night. Josh's lips came down on her neck again and she turned her head slightly to give him more room.

"Hmmm? Am I?"

" 'Fraid so," she whispered, although she did not move or open her eyes as Josh's arm came around her waist to hold her closer to him. A shiver of delightful anticipation went through her.

"I've been good," he pleaded softly. His lips left a fiery trail along her neck, stopping to gently nibble at her ear. "Haven't I?"

"It wasn't nice to laugh at me," she told him. He found a sensitive little hollow beneath her ear and let his lips dance gently there.

"But you were softening," he insisted. His hand moved upward to cup her breast. Even through her bra and cotton shirt, the tip was sensitive to his touch. She sighed with pleasure and rolled over, opening her eyes abruptly when it stopped.

Josh was leaning over her, his hand pulling impatiently at her blouse, freeing it from her jeans so that his hand could slip underneath. After adeptly unhooking her bra, his one hand caressed her soft, smooth skin while the other slid under her neck.

"Admit it," he urged as he leaned forward to tease her lips with tiny little kisses that landed all around her mouth but never quite on it. "You were attracted to me, weren't you?"

"A little," she breathed, reaching up to unbutton his shirt. "Just a little." She ran her fingers slowly through the dark brown hair that covered his chest, the strands of hair curling around her fingers as she felt his skin. It was slightly damp from sweat and tasted of salt as she reached up to tease him with her own kisses.

"Is that so?" he scoffed gently, unbuttoning her blouse and pushing it back from her body. In the soft glow from a ceiling light outside the bathroom, she could see his eyes darken with passion as he looked at her.

Slowly he bent down, placing long warm kisses in the valley between her breasts. The air in the room felt cool on her skin, but his lips left her warm and glowing. Then he took the tip of one breast in his mouth, his lips and tongue playing with it gently until it hardened as her desire increased.

"Just a little, is that what you said?" he asked. He raised his head to laugh slightly, then lowered more of his weight on her as his lips kissed the tender pulse points on her neck.

Tracy's hands slid around his body, her fingers digging into his back as her passion grew and his kisses became less controlled. His weight seemed to be crushing the breath from her body, but it wasn't enough. She needed him closer still.

"I wanted you more than your damned little bit," he said, his voice ragged and hoarse. "God, there was something about you that was driving me crazy. I had to feel you beneath me. Yet every time I tried to get close, that damned conscience got in my way."

"Where is it now?" she asked. Her right hand reached up to touch his face and brush back the hair that had fallen forward.

"Gone. Shot down. Wiped out." He punctuated each sentence with a lingering kiss on her lips.

Soft and warm, they clung to hers longer each time, reluctant to leave. "It disappeared when it decided that you wanted me as much as I wanted you."

"Wise move," she whispered and let her arms wrap around his neck. She pulled him down closer so that their lips merged. As his tongue slipped inside her mouth, he slipped off her to lie next to her on the bed.

She moaned slightly with dissatisfaction, wanting his body smashing hers into the bed, but his hand was tugging at the snap closing her jeans at the waist. It popped open and the zipper slid down in one scandalously eager movement. Tracy's moan became a sigh of pleasure when his hand slid under her lace panties and into the warmth between her thighs.

With movements quick and purposeful, he forced her body to respond to him. Soon every inch of her was aching for him, craving his touch as the last of their clothes found their way to the floor. Tracy needed him with an intensity that she had never experienced before.

She was past words, her breath coming in ragged gasps; she clung shamelessly to him. She was floating, flying, and falling all at the same time as Josh slid his body between her waiting legs. Locked in his arms, she felt her life shatter into a thousand stars. While she drifted back to earth, still safely imprisoned by his strength, her only thought was of how much she loved him.

Chapter Seven

THE SNOWSTORM did not leave the predicted foot and a half of snow on Chicago, but the fourteen inches it did drop was enough to paralyze much of the city and the surrounding area. Although the snow stopped falling by the middle of the morning after Christmas, the wind continued, making it almost impossible to keep the roads clear.

Tracy and Josh left the motel around ten o'clock in the morning. That magical attraction that had driven them to such heights of passion the night before seemed to disappear in the light of day. Josh retreated into a moody silence, while Tracy made a few awkward attempts at conversation, then took to staring out the window.

She knew that they couldn't have stayed in that tiny cabin for long. Cookies and beer were hardly a balanced diet, and they both were starving for some real food. But still, she worried that their relationship might not be strong enough for the realities of everyday life. Or was she kidding herself that there was any relationship at all? She wasn't greatly experienced with one-night stands, but the longer Josh's silence lasted, the more she suspected that that area of her education had just been attended to.

Perhaps fate was trying to make up for the dirty

trick of stranding them the night before: their luck held, and the roads stayed clear for them. They stopped a few times when Tracy wanted to take some pictures and at the single restaurant they found open, a McDonald's in Crystal Lake. Since the restaurant's deliveries had not arrived, the Big Macs had no lettuce, but with French fries and coffee, the food seemed like a feast. Unfortunately, their conversation was stilted and practically nonexistent.

As they drove on, Tracy tried to analyze the reasons for Josh's reticence. Before they had found a place to eat, she had told herself he was hungry. When his silence continued after they had eaten, however, she knew there was only one reason: he was regretting the passion they had shared. Well, she would put his mind at ease. She was not about to force him into any relationship he didn't want.

Tracy did not know whether to be relieved or not when they pulled up to the corner of Broadway and Argyle a little before three o'clock. Her street had not been plowed and this was as close as he could get.

"I'll bet you thought you were never going to get home," Josh joked awkwardly as they got out of the car. He took her bag from the trunk, glancing down the street as he put it down on the sidewalk. Her building was in the middle of the long block. "Want me to carry that for you?" he offered.

"Goodness, no," she laughed brightly. "It's not very heavy, and I don't think you're parked in a very good spot."

She collected her purse and camera case from the car, leaving the cameo and Denise's ring in the white jeweler's box on the front seat. How did one casually say good-bye to a suddenly cooled ardent lover?

"Well, it's been an interesting few days," she said, closing the passenger door of his car as she swung her camera case over her shoulder, and pulling her knitted cap over her hair. Then she walked toward him and her suitcase.

"That's one way to put it," he noted cryptically. A car honked for Josh to move, and he waved impatiently in acknowledgment. When he noticed it was a police car, his wave became a little more agreeable. "I'd better get moving," he said and leaned forward to kiss her quickly on the lips, then hurried around his car. "We'll have dinner tomorrow night," he called with a quick wave before getting in and driving off.

"Yeah, so long," she muttered sarcastically. "I had a wonderful time, too." Not bothering to watch once the car started to move, she picked up her suitcase and trudged as briskly as possible through the snow. She was no fool and could read rejection in a man's eyes. Lord knows, she had seen it there before.

Carefully trying to avoid all thought, she hurried up the narrow path someone had shoveled on the stairs and went into her apartment. A sigh of relief escaped her lips as the door closed behind her.

God, she had been a first-class fool for letting herself get involved with him! She deserved all the misery she knew was coming for being so stupid. Josh had never even pretended to care about her. He just was willing to take what she had been so willing to give.

She took off her coat and tossed it onto the

nearby rack, wishing she could toss off her love for Josh as easily. After dumping her suitcase on her bed, she went into the bathroom and turned on her shower. She'd feel better after she washed her hair and took a shower.

As much as she'd like to place all the blame on Josh, she couldn't even do that, Tracy realized as she went back into the bedroom to get her robe and shampoo from her suitcase. He hadn't forced her into the masquerade. No, she had agreed quite willingly because she had felt sorry for him. She was so dumb! When was she going to stop trying to rescue the world?

She pulled off her pink knitted top and her jeans, leaving them where they fell on the floor. Her bra and panties joined them, then she picked up her robe and shampoo and went into the bathroom. It was steamy, warm, and comforting, and perfect for a good cry, but just as she was about to step into the shower, the phone rang.

"Damn!" she said, hesitating with one foot in the shower and one out. She had a good mind to let it ring. There was no one she really wanted to talk to anyway. Unfortunately, the one person she'd love to speak to popped into her mind.

"It can't be Josh," she scolded herself as she grabbed a towel and ran from the bathroom. "What am I expecting? He's calling because he forgot to tell me he loves me?" In spite of her sarcastic thoughts, her voice was breathless as she picked up the phone.

"Monroe? Where the hell have you been?"

"Hi, Al. Merry Christmas to you too." She couldn't keep the dejection from her voice as she spoke to her boss.

"Christmas is over, Monroe," he pointed out, none too gently. "And we've got a major story breaking."

She shivered in the cool air of the apartment and pulled the towel more tightly around her. "I'm scheduled to come in in the morning," she reminded him. "This is still my day off."

"I don't particularly care," he snapped. "I need you now. You and Bineski are the only cameras I've got and there's only a few hours of daylight left. Got a pencil and paper?"

She sighed and fished some paper out of a drawer beneath the phone. "Go ahead," she said. "But I should warn you, I doubt that I can get my car out."

"That's okay," he assured her. "The main streets are open, so the CTA's running."

Great, she thought as she copied down the addresses and items that he wanted photographed; just what she needed. Trying to find her way around the city by bus should quite effectively remove Josh from her mind.

After changing into clean clothes, Tracy packed up her equipment, ate a quick peanut-butter sandwich, and then left her apartment. The storm was the major story in the news and Al wanted her to photograph its effects. That wasn't too hard to do in any neighborhood, but Al also wanted her to get some contrasting shots: like an unplowed semi-main street with cars paralyzed by the drifts and others of the city trucks plowing out an alderman's tiny residential street.

Then there were definite stories that were already written and needed accompanying pictures. Those were harder because they required more traveling on the erratically running buses, but about half of them were shots of people and could be taken indoors if it was after dark. That gave her a bit more flexibility to look for good shots and not race from one destination to another. She could watch how the city worked and didn't work with as much film as she wanted.

Ever since Mayor Bilandic's reelection defeat had been blamed on his poor handling of a heavy snowstorm, every snowfall in Chicago had become a political issue. Each faction of Democrats (there were virtually no Republicans in Chicago) was quick to criticize or praise the snow-removal crews depending on who was in office, yet the citizens were really the only judges of how well the streets were cleaned and how quickly things got back to normal. This was what Tracy liked to show: how the city was really working, not how various political groups claimed it was.

After hours on the streets, Tracy finally made her way back to the newspaper. She developed the rolls of film that she had taken in the city as well as the ones she had taken on their way back from Harvard, and made copies of all the prints. Some were her own personal photos, and those she put away.

Most of them were pictures of the storm, though, and there were a number of excellent shots. Huge snowdrifts dwarfing snowplows. Semis practically buried in the snow. A tow truck that got stalled in the snow while trying to pull a car out. The subjects were common enough in any storm, but Tracy thought the composition and clarity of her shots made them better than the average.

Al seemed to think so, too. After choosing a few shots for the next edition, he took a more leisurely perusal of the others. "They're good, Monroe," he told her. "You've got a real eye for a shot." Tracy smiled wearily at the praise as he passed the photos back to her and stood up. "Stick around, I may have to send you out again."

So much for praise, Tracy thought, picking up her pictures. She felt exhausted and the idea of going out on another story was far from pleasant, but neither was the thought of making her way home on the buses at night. She packed her photos into an envelope and got to her feet. That old sofa in the lounge down the hall would be just the thing if someone hadn't already beaten her to it.

Tracy was hardly looking or feeling her best when Josh came over to the picture desk a little after nine the next morning. She had been called out in the middle of the night to photograph a fire, and then had to crop and blow up the pictures three times until layout was satisfied. Finally able to relax, she had gotten herself a cup of coffee and had just sat down when she saw Josh approach Al's desk.

She knew her face lit up and her smile must surely have wiped away some of the signs of weariness, but Josh did not even look her way.

"I need a photographer," he said briskly to Al.

Tracy's smile faded as he continued to ignore her. It had to be that, for he was not more than ten feet away from her. How could he not have seen her?

"Take your pick," Al shrugged, looking up

from some paperwork. "I've got Bineski or Monroe."

Josh turned to look at her then, but his glance was cool and impersonal as his eyes went from her to where Bob Bineski was putting away some equipment in his locker. Was he trying to tease her? she wondered.

"Doesn't matter," he said, turning back to Al.

It didn't matter! Tracy could not believe her ears. If she had had any doubts about Josh's desire to continue their relationship, they were gone now. Well, if he could play it cool, so could she.

"I'll go, Al," she said lightly, standing up and downing the rest of her coffee. "Bob just got back from his assignment and is ready to drop on his feet." She turned to Josh, her manner professional and businesslike. "Want to wait here while I get my things?"

"No, that won't be necessary," he assured her and pulled a paper from his pocket. "This is for a story on the poor quality in some recently built city and county buildings. I've got a list here of the buildings and specific places I need pictures of." He handed her the list. "I think you should find everything without any trouble." Without another word, he turned and walked away.

Tracy felt like throwing something large and heavy at him as she watched him disappear around a corner. How could he treat her as if they were virtual strangers? Obviously the other night had meant nothing to him.

"Something wrong?"

She jumped slightly and turned to find Al watching her.

"No," she forced herself to laugh. "I was just

checking to see if I knew how to get to all these places. I'd hate to end up on the wrong bus or at the wrong building.''

''Well, hopefully, Reilly'll be in to replace you by the time you get back,'' Al told her. ''But I doubt that he'll be willing to convince Rettinger that the County Courthouse is the Dirksen Building. He tries to avoid the man whenever possible.''

Tracy frowned as she slipped the list into her pocket. ''I thought I was the only one who couldn't get along with him.''

Al laughed and took a drink of the cold coffee on his desk. ''You and the rest of the world, Monroe.'' His phone rang and he turned aside.

Tracy did not find it particularly comforting to know that Josh's dislike was not personal, but she forced all thought of it from her mind as she went out on the assignment. Lenses, lighting, and proper angles were all that mattered. And actually, by the time she got back to the paper, she was too tired to wrestle with the problem anyway.

After developing the pictures, she walked wearily into the city room. Bob Bineski passed her in the doorway.

''Did Al tell you McGovern and Reilly finally got here so we can go home?'' he asked her.

''Hurrah,'' she smiled wearily. ''I'm not sure I've got the strength to get home, though.''

He laughed as he buttoned his coat. ''What you need is food,'' he told her. ''Some of us are going over to Billy Goat's for some lunch. Want to join us?''

She held up the envelope of pictures. ''Got to make a delivery first, but then I might. I need something before I face the buses again.''

Bob nodded and went down the hall. Bob was probably right, she thought as she wove through the maze of desks over to Josh's. She ought to have something to eat before she went home. Then she'd have no reason to wake up for the next twenty-four hours.

She was yawning as she got to his desk. She had half-hoped that he might be out on a story and she wouldn't need to feel his rejection again, but he was sitting there, paging through his notes and entering them in the computer terminal on his desk.

With a businesslike briskness that she was proud of, she tossed the photographs on his desk. He glanced up with a nod, barely pausing in his work.

About to turn around without a word, Tracy stopped for some reason. "Some of us are going over to Billy Goat's for lunch. Want to come along?"

He didn't even pause in his work. "No, thanks."

Tracy's shrug of careful nonchalance was a masterpiece of acting and she never did know how she kept the tears from falling until she reached her apartment.

A persistent knocking kept bothering Tracy, waking her slightly from the sleep she was reluctant to leave. Finally she opened her eyes and stared ahead of her in the darkness. The knocking continued.

With a sigh, she sat up in bed and reached over to turn on the light next to her bed. She still had on her robe, but the towel she had wrapped around her wet hair had fallen to the floor. Her feet found it as she looked at the clock. It was just past seven.

Lord, she felt just as exhausted now as she had when she went to bed five hours ago, she thought as she rose slowly to her feet. The knocking continued.

"I'm coming! I'm coming!" she shouted to the knocker, who couldn't possibly have heard her for he was making so much noise.

She walked through the hallway and into the living room, running her fingers through her hair and realizing how hungry she was. She should have gone to Billy Goat's or someplace before she came home. If she remembered correctly, there wasn't much beyond peanut butter in the house.

Switching on a light as she went by, Tracy reached up to unbolt the door. "Who's there?" she asked sleepily.

"It's me, Josh."

Her surprise was so great that she wondered how she got the door open, but she did, and sure enough, there was Josh standing outside with a worried frown on his face.

"What took you so long? I was worried that something had happened," he said as he stepped into the apartment.

The shock wore off suddenly. "What the hell are you doing here?" she snapped as he moved toward her, seemingly planning to kiss her.

Her words effectively stopped him. "We had a date tonight, remember?" His voice reflected his confusion as his eyes took in her mussed hair and sleep-swollen eyes. "If you're too tired, we don't have to go out."

Consideration for her was not her first interpretation. "No, you'd like that, wouldn't you? Just a quick jump into bed with the idiot, and then off you'll go without having taken the risk that someone might see you." Her eyes were flashing fiercely as all her pain came back.

"What are you talking about?" His frown was not particularly patient, but she refused to notice.

"You know very well what I'm talking about," she insisted haughtily, crossing her arms over her chest. Her diminutive height lessened the effectiveness, however. "I'm onto your little game and I refuse to play any longer."

He looked rather angry at her words, but he bit off a curse and turned around, slowly taking his coat off. After draping it over the back of a chair, he walked a few feet away from her and then turned to face her once more. "Now would you mind telling me in plain English what is wrong?"

"What is there to explain?" she cried, not trying to conceal the tears that suddenly began to run down her cheeks. "I was an idiot yesterday, but I won't be again. When I get involved with another man, he won't be ashamed to be seen with me."

Josh sighed and took a step toward her. "Tracy, I'm trying, but I don't know what you're talking about. Is this because I wouldn't go to Billy Goat's with you?"

"Oh, it wasn't just that," she said with disgust. She wiped the tears from her cheeks, and turned away from him. "I could see that you didn't want anyone at work to know that we had spent Christmas together. Well, that's fine with me, but you shouldn't come around here expecting that I'll go along with your secret affair." She jumped suddenly as his arms went around her from behind.

"So that's how your mind works," he said quietly, kissing her neck just below her right ear.

An unwanted shiver of excitement went through her, but she did not move away.

"I am sorry if I hurt you," he told her softly while planting gentle kisses all along the base of her neck. "It was the last thing in the world I ever wanted to do. You have to believe me."

When he held her in his arms, she would believe anything that he wanted, she realized, and pulled away from him, wiping her eyes with her sleeve.

"Does that Chinese restaurant down the street have good food?" he asked suddenly.

She turned to stare at him. "It's pretty good," she said.

He leaned forward to kiss her quickly. "Fine, I'll go get us some dinner and bring it here. You go get dressed and stop crying. We'll talk after we eat."

"I don't know that we have anything to talk about," she pointed out stubbornly.

He reached out and took her hand. "Tracy, don't," he said softly. "We hardly know one another. Don't let a stupid misunderstanding spoil things."

She still was rather suspicious of his motives, but agreed to his request. Not that it was going to change her mind, she assured herself as she put on a deep-purple velour jumpsuit with long full sleeves and a gold belt. It fit snugly over her trim hips, and the knowledge that she looked good gave her confidence. He was not going to find some weak little woman, begging for his favors.

By the time Josh returned, she had removed all

traces of her earlier tears and had put on a light covering of makeup. Her hair was neatly combed, and she was very much in control of herself as she scooped up her suitcase and dirty clothes, and dumped them on her closet floor. She disliked a messy room, she assured herself as she hurried to let Josh back in.

"You look a little more awake," he teased her gently and handed her several bags filled with little white cardboard containers. They felt warm in her arms, but her eyes were cool as she watched Josh take his coat off and hang it up.

"I was awake enough before," she said crisply.

Josh sighed impatiently. "This isn't getting us very far."

She just shrugged and carried the food into the kitchen. There were a few dishes already on the table, so she unpacked the bags, looking into each little box to see what else she would need.

"You have to understand that this caring about somebody else is new to me," he told her with some embarrassment.

Her heart softened slightly toward him, but she refused to let it show as she got two more bowls from the cabinet. "Oh, come off it, Josh," she argued. "When you care about someone, you say hello to them. You ask them how they are. Little things like that."

"I didn't have to ask," he snapped as he sat down at the table. "I could see you were exhausted from working all night."

"All from one glance?" she mocked. "Just where was it written on my face that I had been there all night?"

He dumped an order of rice into a bowl. "I

knew because I had been calling your apartment for hours last night and was worried when you didn't answer. I was about to come back up here, when I called the paper and learned that you had gone into work."

"Oh." She removed two hot egg rolls from a bag and carefully laid them on a plate with two packets of sweet-sour sauce. "Why didn't you say something, then?" she asked, but her voice was far less aggressive.

Josh reached across and took a container of Szechwan shrimp out of her hand, then pulled her over to where he sat. "Tracy, I'm a private person," he said quietly, looking up into her soft blue eyes. "I don't want everyone in the world, or the office, to know everything I do."

She tried to pull her hand away from his. He let it go, only to rise to his feet and put his hands on her upper arms. "I have never been able to be friends with the people I work with, and I don't really want to. To do my job well, I need to concentrate and work hard and be suspicious of everybody. That includes the people I work with who aren't always as careful in their research as they should be, or who hold back a single bit of information because they want credit for the whole story. I can't be one person with them and a different one with you. I can only be one person at work and a different one when we're alone. If you can't handle that, then go start up with someone like Al."

"Al? You're crazy!" she laughed. "He's in his late forties and has a grandchild."

"So?" Josh's eyebrows raised. "There already
137

are rumors that you're sleeping with him. He might like to make them true.''

"Me and Al?" she cried, pulling away from him in astonishment. ''But that's ridiculous.''

"Of course it is, but he'd probably be happy to fuss over you and coddle you in front of everybody. If you want to take a chance with me, though, you won't get that.'' He tried to make her understand. "We'll just be two different people. A reporter and a photographer who occasionally work with each other, and then us.''

Tracy said nothing for a long moment, walking slowly back to the table and folding up the two empty bags. "Why didn't you say all this in the car when we were coming back?" she asked him quietly. "Why did you let me think you didn't want to see me anymore?''

"Is that what you were thinking?" he laughed and walked over behind her, putting his arms around her. While one hand slid possessively over her flat stomach, the other reached up to caress her breast. "I guess I didn't know how to say it. Or whether you would even want to see me once we were back.'' His lips kissed the side of her neck.

Tracy turned in his arms, sliding her own arms up around his neck and pressing her body close to his. "I guess we were both a little silly," she acknowledged. The top few buttons of his shirt were unbuttoned and she planted a teasing little kiss on his chest.

"I take it I'm forgiven for being so unfriendly?" he asked with a smile.

"Only if you forgive me for being so sensitive," she said.

Bending down to meet her lips, he smiled gently at her. "I'll consider a suitable punishment," he whispered.

His lips were warm and soft and deliciously demanding as they devoured hers. Moving roughly over her mouth, they told her of his desperate longing for her and of his passion that grew with each breath.

His touch held a potent magic that seeped into her soul as his caresses grew slower and more forceful. All over her back his hands roamed, more than just touching, for his fingers seemed to set her skin aflame. Rather, his hands were pushing and molding, crushing her body ever closer to his, while they left a searing trail in their wake.

Tracy felt stunned by his sensual onslaught and barely capable of coherent thought. Her need for him was as overpowering as his was for her and this time there was no place for flirting and being coy. Waves of desire were cascading through her body and her only thought was of fulfillment.

Josh removed his lips reluctantly from hers and took a deep breath as Tracy laid her head against his chest. With her tongue, she tickled the little hollows in his throat.

"Can Chinese food be reheated?" he asked with a desperate edge to his voice. "Or do we throw it out and eat later?"

Tracy laughed quietly. She had found a particularly sensitive spot on his neck and enjoyed the tremor of excitement that she felt race through him.

"Tracy," he groaned, and held her slightly away from him. "What do we do with the food?"

She just shrugged, her eyes lit with a passionate gleam. "We can heat it up in the microwave when we're ready to eat. If we ever are," she added, squirming to break his hold and get closer to him again. He could not fight her for long.

"So what do we do with it now?" he asked as his lips found an equally sensitive spot on her neck. She trembled in his arms, clinging to him blindly as her desire raged almost out of control. "Can we leave it out?"

Tracy blinked up at him dazedly. The sudden explosion of her desire had left her confused. "No," she said hoarsely. "I guess it had better go in the refrigerator."

She pulled away from him slowly, passion having drugged her mind and her body. But once away from his embrace, the need to return to it was so strong that her movements became quicker. The food was dumped into the refrigerator, and before the door swung shut, Josh had swept her up into his arms.

"Have you noticed how perfectly matched we are?" he murmured as her arms tightened around his neck. He bent down to kiss the valley between her breasts that was exposed by the low neckline of her jumpsuit.

"Hmmm?" she sighed, reveling in the feel of his lips on her skin.

"We have so many interests in common." His voice was teasing as he stopped in the doorway of her bedroom. She reached around him to flick on the light, thankful that she had cleaned the room.

"So many interesting ways to pass the time," he said softly as he laid her on the bed.

Her arms were still around his neck and she pulled him down next to her. The fire of their passion flared up, consuming them with its raging intensity.

Chapter Eight

"THESE ARE really super pictures," Tom Davenport exclaimed enthusiastically.

"Thanks a lot." Tracy smiled gently. Tom was a young reporter, not long out of school, who had been working the last few days in the city room. Although he seemed nice enough, he was terribly inexperienced and most of the other reporters had little patience with his lack of professionalism and pathetic eagerness to please.

He didn't bother Tracy, though, because he reminded her of a large, overeager puppy. It wasn't just his manner; he actually looked like one with his untidy hair and clumsy movements. Feeling sorry for him, she had offered to take the assignment today before the other photographers had a chance to refuse, although she would have much preferred working with Josh.

It was only a week since they had returned from his parents' home, and she still wanted to be with him constantly. She felt rather like a schoolgirl waiting at her locker for hours so that she could just "happen" to be there when that one special boy walked by, but she couldn't help it. Even though he had not budged on his "separate people at work" rule, she still felt tense and excited when she happened to see him.

''You're really a great photographer,'' Tom went on, paging through the shots again and dragging her mind from Josh. ''I've never seen pictures this good.''

Tracy suspected that the real reason for his enthusiasm and praise was that she had been less critical of him. The bank robbery that he had been assigned to cover had been a routine story and her accompanying pictures were quite adequate, but it wasn't as if she had caught the robbers in action or anything. He must have decided that she was his friend.

She turned to move away from his desk, but he hurried after her. ''I hope we'll be working together again soon,'' he told her quietly.

''I don't see how we can avoid it,'' she pointed out. ''There aren't that many photographers around.''

He shrugged. ''Well, I'm only here temporarily from the suburban news page. You've got so many reporters out with the flu that they called me to fill in.

''But this is where I really want to work someday,'' he added eagerly. ''So if you could put in a good word for me . . .''

Tracy laughed and patted Tom's arm. ''I doubt that anyone would listen,'' she told him. ''It's your writing that counts.''

He nodded, but did not seem to have much confidence on that score. ''It ought to, but some of those other guys would be sure to get me out of here if they had the chance,'' he complained. He glanced around the city room rather furtively. ''Take that Rettinger, for instance. He really hates me.''

Tracy could not help but look up and found Josh glaring at her. She turned back to Tom. "Oh, you can't take that personally," she assured him with a smile. "He hates everybody."

Tom looked disbelieving and continued to follow her as she tried to move away again. "Say, I was wondering if you were free tonight," he asked her suddenly. "Maybe we could have a drink or something."

He looked so hopeful that she hated to refuse but she shook her head with a kind smile. "I'm really sorry," she said. "I already have plans."

"I might have known," he grumbled dejectedly. "But if he stands you up, remember my offer."

"I will," she assured him as heavy footsteps approached from behind her.

"If you're quite done, Miss Monroe, I've been waiting for a photographer for some time now," Josh said coldly.

Tracy turned around to face him. Her lips were solemn, but her eyes laughed at him. "Why, certainly. Shall I get my equipment and meet you at the elevators?"

"No, I'll go with you," he announced to her surprise.

She turned, noticing that Tom had disappeared, and walked out of the city room to her locker in the hallway. It was deserted and Josh leaned against the one next to hers.

"If you want to go out with him tonight, I'll understand," he told her solemnly.

She just stared up at him for a moment. "Why would I want to do that?" she blurted out.

"Well, you seemed to enjoy his company,"

145

Josh pointed out. "And you probably have a lot in common with him—"

Tracy's eyes narrowed suspiciously as he spoke. "What day is this?" she interrupted him, her voice ripe with irritation. "The feast of St. Joshua the martyr?"

Josh looked affronted and stood up straight. "I was only trying—"

"Look," she snapped. "If you want to get rid of me, say so and I won't bother you again. But don't try to foist me off on some overeager puppy."

She slammed her locker shut, and pulled her jacket on. Josh stood in the hallway, glaring at her. "I'll meet you downstairs," he said.

"Fine," she snapped back as he turned around to get his things.

By the time she rode down in the elevator, Tracy's anger had cooled. He was jealous, that was all, and it was a good sign. She just had to be calmer and not fly into anger every time he got huffy. She had the distinct feeling that he was going to resist love for a long time, and it was going to be up to her to exercise the patience needed.

He was waiting for her when she got down to the lobby. His face was controlled and serious, and they left the building in silence.

He hurried across the street, oblivious to the puddles of slush everywhere that her feet seemed to find. Racing after him, Tracy had the feeling that she had done all this before. "What assignment do you have?" she finally called to him.

He turned to see her hurrying after him, and slowed his step. "I wanted to interview more of those office workers in the county building department, and need pictures to go with them.''

Tracy frowned at him. ''But we interviewed dozens of people yesterday and you said that was a waste of time.''

''I thought we might get something better today,'' he shrugged and turned to flag down a cab.

''But you interviewed everyone in a position to have the information,'' she persisted, hurrying alongside him and keeping her eyes on his face.

''All right, damnit!'' Josh cried suddenly as a cab stopped next to them and he pulled open the door. ''So I didn't have an assignment. I just didn't like the way he was pawing you!''

''He wasn't pawing me,'' she protested quietly. ''He was telling me how you hate him.''

Josh shrugged as they got into the cab. He turned away from her to tell the driver their destination, but then was glaring at her again. ''He's right, I do. I hate anybody that you smile at.''

''No, you don't,'' she laughed, taking his arm and leaning her head against it. ''You're just jealous because I don't smile at you at work, but it's your rule, you know. Change it if you want to.''

He glanced at the driver, who was pretending to be interested only in the oncoming traffic. Then, with a sudden groan, Josh pulled her into his arms and kissed her hungrily. His lips demanded an immediate response as his tongue pushed its way into her mouth.

He was hurt and confused and needed the reassurance that only her mouth could give him. ''God, you are driving me crazy,'' he whispered so only she could hear. His breath was soft and warm on her lips. ''I can't seem to get enough of you.''

She reached up and gently stroked his face as if she could erase the lines of worry that time had left there. "Hey, just because I feel sorry for that kid, nothing will change between us."

"I wish I could believe that," he said, looking deep into her eyes with something that looked almost like fear in his. "But I keep remembering that this all started because you felt sorry for me. What if you meet him in some bar and feel compelled to take him home?"

"I'm not stupid," she laughed gently at him. "I can only handle so many strays at a time. I've learned to close my heart to all others when my house is full."

"And is it now?"

She reached up to kiss his lips slowly, with a promise of the passion that they would share later. "It's full and the door is locked," she assured him softly. "To keep out and to keep in."

As her lips went up to his again, his arms went around her, pulling her closer and closer. Even as his embrace tightened, though, she sensed him relaxing slightly. His hands caressed her with desire, the anger and fear gone.

Suddenly, he released her with a long sigh as the cab jerked to a stop. "Here's the County Building, buddy," the cab driver said with a smirk. Josh shoved the money into his hand, and hurried Tracy out of the cab.

Josh pulled his car into the parking space with a frown. It must be the weather that was depressing him so, he thought as he got of his car. It was only the third week of January, so there were two more months of rotten weather ahead. That would be enough to depress anybody.

He climbed up the steps to Tracy's apartment and rang her bell. His mental attitude had nothing to do with the fact that she was flying down to Florida for a long weekend, he assured himself. He was not so attached to her that he couldn't live without her for a few days.

Actually it was a relief that she was going, he thought as he rang the bell again. He had a number of things that needed doing around his apartment that he had neglected as of late. And she had become rather demanding. Oh, not in actual words, but somehow she had entangled him in her affairs, and this was a good time to reestablish his independence.

"Oh, Josh," Tracy cried when she opened the door. "I'm not going to be able to go." She looked so unhappy that he forced back the sudden surge of joy that her words caused.

"What do you mean you're not going?" he asked, moving her gently aside so he could enter. "Don't your parents want you to come down this weekend?"

"It's not them," she sighed. "I've got another cat."

Josh took his coat off and tossed it onto a nearby chair in exasperation. "What happened? I thought you had managed to get rid of all the animals."

She shrugged as she closed the door behind him. "This one was pregnant and just abandoned. None of their other homes could take her and they were getting desperate. What could I say?"

"How about no for a change?" He was less than patient with her.

149

She smiled weakly and sat on the edge of a chair facing him. "I tried to reach you before you left so you wouldn't come out here for nothing," she explained. A stray tear rolled down her cheek. "I mean, I don't need a ride to the airport if I'm not going on a trip." Another tear rolled down and she brushed it away irritably.

"Oh, Tracy, Tracy, Tracy," Josh sighed. He came over and pulled her up into his arms so she could cry comfortably. "Why on earth don't you just go on your trip if you want to so badly?"

"I can't leave Cookie," she sobbed. "She's due any time now."

Josh patted her back soothingly. "You think she can't have her kittens without you?" he teased gently. "Cats have been having kittens for a long time before anybody ever thought of you."

He felt her nod, but she said nothing.

"Hey, if I stay here and baby-sit Cookie, then will you go on your trip?" he offered.

Tracy pulled away from him. "You?" she said, sounding stunned. "But what do you know about pregnant cats?"

He made a wry face. "I grew up on a farm, remember? We had dozens of cats who were constantly having kittens." He tried not to smile at the picture his words conjured up.

"But that was different," she insisted. "Besides, you're not the dummy that agreed to take Cookie. This is my responsibility and I have to handle it."

Josh frowned. She had been so excited about visiting her parents that it had annoyed him slightly, but now that her trip was in jeopardy, he could not bear to see her disappointed. "You are going on that trip if I have to put you in an envelope and mail you,'' he declared. ''I insist!''

Tracy stepped back from him. Her frown and glare indicated her state of mind. ''You insist?''

He nodded, unconcerned about her growing anger. ''It's a matter of honor,'' he explained blithely. ''Ever since you agreed to that masquerade over Christmas, I've been in your debt. If you don't accept this trip that I'm paying for, I will never feel like an equal partner in our relationship.''

Tracy just stared at him. ''But Cookie . . .''

''I can take care of Cookie,'' he swept aside her arguments. ''You settle our debt.''

She continued to stare at him. ''Well, if you're sure . . .''

''Of course I am,'' he said quickly. ''Now get your bag or you'll miss the plane.''

The trip to O'Hare Airport was filled with last-minute instructions and explanations of where everything was located in her apartment. Josh just kept nodding, although his mind actually was taking in little that she was saying; for the closer they got to the airport, the more dejected he felt. Damn, he was going to miss her!

''I don't have to go,'' she said when he pulled up at the Delta departure gate. ''It's not too late.''

''Have a great time,'' he said, pulling her over to him for a kiss. Her lips felt so good on his that he should have just enjoyed the moment, but all he could think about was that it would be three days before he kissed her again.

''I will,'' she smiled. She opened her door and a redcap came hurrying over to take her luggage. A minute later, after a quick wave, she was inside the building and lost to his sight.

Damn! What was the matter with him? he thought as he drove away. They were having a fun, casual relationship, nothing serious. Why the hell did he want to follow her and beg her not to go?

After turning up the radio to drown out his thoughts, Josh drove to his apartment. He got some clothes and other essentials, such as a six-pack of beer and her picture, and returned to Tracy's apartment.

It seemed so damned empty without her, just like the next three days that stretched out endlessly before him. How would he ever fill the time?

He dumped his clothes in her bedroom and carried his beer out to the kitchen, where a black-and-white cat lay in a newspaper-lined box.

''Well, Cookie,'' he said, opening one of his cans. ''It looks like it's just you and me for the next few days.''

He raised his can in a mock toast and then took a long drink, stopping when he heard a strange noise. Cookie was not paying attention to him: she had other things on her mind just then.

''Swell,'' he muttered, squatting down to take a look. ''I guess it won't be just you and me.''

Tracy opened her eyes slowly and looked over at the man sleeping next to her. He looked very different in repose. With his usual cynical air gone from his face, the gentleness and compassion that he kept so hidden could be seen.

In the past six weeks, Tracy had come to know Josh much better, growing to love him more each day. He was still very reserved and hesitant about expressing his feelings, but she could read much more in his eyes than he was aware of.

She reached over and gently stroked the streaks of gray that highlighted his temples, keeping her touch light so as not to wake him. He had become very important to her, but the thought of the future worried her. She knew that she needed him in hers; but did he feel the same about her?

She withdrew her hand and quietly eased herself out of bed. After wrapping her robe around her shoulders, she walked barefoot out of the bedroom. Cookie greeted her at the kitchen door, ignoring the crying of her two-week-old kittens.

Monica must have hurt Josh a great deal, Tracy thought as she took her coffeepot out of a cabinet and filled it with water. It was hard to believe that anyone could care enough about Monica to be hurt by her, but Josh's fear of commitment certainly seemed to stem from his marriage. She wondered what the real reason for his divorce had been. After all, if two people really loved each other they would make compromises. Monica's dislike of Chicago should not have been that big a problem.

After measuring the coffee into the basket, Tracy plugged in the pot and began to set the table for breakfast. The problem was that Josh was such a loner and she didn't know why. Did he prefer being alone or had he chosen it because it seemed safer than risking love?

During the past six weeks there had not been a real strengthening of their relationship. The only place they really communicated was in bed, and she was so afraid that she was reading more into his passion than he felt. Yet his eyes were so gentle and tender. . . .

Tracy stopped her meandering thoughts and turned to the refrigerator and took out bacon, eggs, and milk. It did no good to go over and over things, she told herself as she put a frying pan on the stove and turned on the heat.

If she had learned nothing else about Josh in the past weeks, she had learned that he was afraid to get close. It was obvious in so many little ways. He never said he loved her; yet he could be more tender and considerate than David ever was. He still wanted to hide their relationship from the people at the paper, but he got so upset when one of the pressmen was flirting with her. He wanted to be with her constantly, but refused to consider living together.

It was quite possible, she knew, that he was just using her, that she had read all sorts of romantic motives into his actions only because she wanted them to be there. But she was willing to take the risk. If he left she would want to die, for she loved him more than she ever thought possible; but if he learned to trust her love enough to love her back, their life together would be happiness beyond belief. She just had to be patient and give him time.

''Why didn't you wake me up?''

Tracy turned around from the cooking bacon to see Josh frowning at her from the doorway.

''Morning,'' she smiled and went over to kiss him.

His kiss was hardly passionate: he seemed more interested in buckling his belt. ''You know I never meant to spend the night,'' he reminded her curtly.

She went back to the bacon and turned each slice carefully. "You were exhausted," she told him. "And needed the rest."

He sighed impatiently, but she refused to notice. "I think the coffee must be done," she said cheerfully.

He took a cup from the table and filled it, then stirred in some milk and sugar. "I've got to get home and change," he pointed out. "I should have left hours ago."

"I know, I know," Tracy said wearily. "We've been through this all before." She took out another pan and put in a blob of margarine, watching it slowly slide across the pan as it melted. "The problem is I'm selfish. I like having you next to me when I sleep. I like waking up with you still there. So next time you'd better bring your alarm clock if you really want to go home."

Josh came up behind her and put his arms around her. He kissed the side of her neck. "I'm sorry," he said quietly. "It's not fair to you, I know. You should just tell me to go to hell, and find yourself some nice guy who'll treat you like you deserve."

Hiding the dejection that his comments had caused, she turned in his arms to smile up at him. "Fat chance, buddy. You're stuck with me. You ought to know by now how I feel about you."

He looked over her shoulder at the empty pan. "Speaking of feelings, I'm starving," he joked.

She forced a smile on her face. "Well, then, unhand me and I'll get something cooked." With a smile, he obeyed her command, and she busied herself with the eggs. "How about fixing me some coffee?" she called over her shoulder.

So he wasn't ready to hear that she loved him; what difference did that make? she asked herself sternly as she broke the eggs into a bowl. She had to give him time, she had to be patient. Someday she could tell him that she loved him. Someday he'd want to hear.

She beat the eggs briskly, as if doing so would keep the tears from falling. Surprisingly it worked; and by the time he handed her a steaming cup of coffee, her emotions were back under control. She loved him enough to wait.

Chapter Nine

TRACY SAT ON the edge of her bed and fought the dizziness that threatened to overcome her. Just when she thought it might be safe to slide her feet over a few inches into her slippers, the phone began to ring.

"Great," she muttered sarcastically. Two gray-and-black kittens stopped attacking Cookie's tail to stare at her as she stood up. Clinging determinedly to the furniture along the way, Tracy finally made it across the room to pick up the phone on the fifth ring.

"Hi, beautiful." The sound of Josh's voice made her feel almost alive. "Did I wake you up?"

"No, but it sounds like a great way to wake up," she answered, trying to force some life into her voice even though her legs were wobbling beneath her. She eased herself slowly to the floor. "How's Washington?"

"Lousy," he grumbled. "I wish you had come with me. This is a hell of a way to spend Valentine's Day."

She just laughed. "I promise to make it up to you when you get back. Any idea when that'll be?"

"Who knows?" he sighed. "Nobody wants to be interviewed about James Carlton. I guess they figure that as long as he wants to set up shop in Chicago, they can forget he ever existed. And the public records of some of his real-estate deals will take days to decipher. There's no way I'll be back before the end of the week, at least," he ended morosely.

Maybe that would give her time to join the living again, she thought, changing her position slightly. Unfortunately, the move caused her stomach to rise up in rebellion.

"Tracy?" Josh's voice was worried at her unexpected silence. "Are you all right?"

"Yeah, fine," she assured him, gulping back the nausea. "I think I've got the flu. See how well I timed it, though. Waited until you were out of town." She hoped her weak laugh hid how awful she really felt.

"Are you sure you're okay?" he asked suspiciously. "Maybe you should go see a doctor."

"Yeah, if I'm not better tomorrow, I will," she promised. The room was dancing around her as she stood back up on her shaky feet. "But I think I'd better get back to bed," she said with rising panic. "I'll talk to you later."

She heard a worried "Tracy!" as she hung up the phone, but there was no way that she could talk anymore. It was even too late to go back to bed, and she made a dash for the bathroom, getting there just in time to be sick.

A few minutes later, after rinsing her face with cold water, Tracy realized that she felt a lot better. It was the same as yesterday—she was sick in the morning but fine the rest of the day. She hung up the towel she had used and walked back to her bedroom. What kind of flu made you sick only in the mornings? she wondered with a frown.

Suddenly, realization hit her. Oh, my God, she couldn't be, could she? Hurrying over to her dresser, she rummaged through her top drawer for her calendar and scanned the last few months anxiously. Good Lord, she hadn't had a period since the middle of December. It was now mid-February. Was she pregnant?

"Well, congratulations, Tracy. You're into your second month already."

Still in the state of shock that had started that morning after Josh's phone call, Tracy was only vaguely conscious of the young doctor sitting across his desk from her. She stared at the plants behind him and the pictures of his wife and children, thinking that they looked the same as they had the last time she was in this office several years ago. Was she really back here in Prentiss Women's Hospital? Had time stood still? No; his news was very different this time.

"But how?" she asked, turning her attention to him suddenly. "You told me I couldn't."

Dr. Myers shook his head as he paged through the papers in her file. "No. I said it was unlikely," he corrected her gently. "But as long as that one tube was partially open, there was always a chance of pregnancy. Maybe only one egg every couple of years would manage to get through, but if that egg is fertilized, you're pregnant. However, any woman can have sex at the optimum time in her cycle and still not get pregnant, so your odds were not very good."

Tracy turned to stare out the window, although

there was little she could see beyond the outline of another building that was part of the Northwestern University Medical Center. The thin white blinds obscured its details, just as her mind seemed obscured from reality.

"Is this pregnancy a problem, Tracy?" he asked gently.

Turning back to him, she found his dark eyes watching her sympathetically. "I thought your husband wanted a child."

Her lips twitched slightly with sarcastic appreciation. "My husband has a child," she pointed out. "In fact, he and his present wife may have several by this time. We've been divorced for three years now," she added curtly.

He glanced at the paper before him. "Right after you learned about your blocked tubes?"

She nodded, suddenly feeling guilty for her sarcasm. Dr. Myers was kind and only trying to help her. "This comes as quite a shock," she said quietly. "I had always assumed that I couldn't get pregnant and had finally adjusted myself to that fact."

"What about the baby's father?"

Tracy looked down at her hands. What about Josh? she wondered. How would he react to the news? Would it eliminate his fear of commitment or was it still too early in their relationship, so that his reaction would be a quick departure?

"I don't know," she admitted reluctantly. "We've never discussed the possibility."

"You don't have to have the baby," he pointed out. "It's still early enough to terminate the pregnancy."

Her bones chilled at his words. Is that what it

would come to: a choice between Josh and their baby? "No, I don't want that," she said quickly. "This could be my only chance to have a child, couldn't it?"

He nodded. "It was unlikely that you would get pregnant ever. To hope for a second pregnancy would be expecting a miracle, I'm afraid."

She smiled bravely. "Then I'll just have to hope for the best," she said and rose to her feet.

The morning sickness usually disappeared by mid-morning and, aside from it, Tracy was feeling almost as good as new. Worry about telling Josh kept her from feeling perfect, though, or from really enjoying the knowledge that she was pregnant.

As long as Josh was in Washington, she felt safe. It wasn't the sort of news you would tell a person over the phone, so she kept their conversations cheery, constantly assuring him that she was fine and completely over the flu.

But when he returned early the next week, she went to meet his airplane with mixed feelings. Loving him so, the time without him had been empty and meaningless, yet now that he was returning, she was afraid.

What if he didn't want the baby? What if he only wanted a casual affair with her and wasn't interested in any future? In time she had hoped to make him need her as much as she needed him. Not just in the physical sense, either, but in every possible way. She had hoped that their lives would become so entwined that there would be no possible thought of a life without the other. Yet she was afraid that she hadn't had enough time.

She could wait another month or two to tell him, of course, but would that really be fair? She doubted she could take the uncertainty anyway. The fear of what he would say had to be worse than his rejection would be.

As she watched his plane taxi to the gate, she planned the evening ahead. Much as she would like to blurt out the truth, she wouldn't. If the worst happened and he wanted nothing to do with her and the baby, she would have this one evening to remember.

"Tracy!"

Coming out of her thoughts with a start, Tracy turned around to see Josh hurrying toward her. Even though there were many other people getting off the plane, some being greeted with hugs and kisses and others just trying to hurry through the crowd, he was the only one she saw. God, how she loved him! she realized suddenly as tears came to her eyes. She flew into his embrace with a feeling of desperation. How many more times would he hold her like this?

Dropping the briefcase he carried at his side, Josh held her tightly. A harried, middle-aged woman dragging two crying children bumped into them, but neither of them noticed.

"Damn! It's good to be home," he sighed, burying his face in the curve of her neck and shoulder. Her face was so hidden that he kissed the only part of her that he could find. With a frustrated laugh, he finally held her away from him slightly so that he could look at her face. "Hey, what's the matter?" he asked with a sudden frown.

"I'm just so glad to see you," she said, feeling rather foolish for her tears. "I missed you so much!"

He looked down at her, a slight smile curving his lips. "Good!" he teased. "I'd hate to think I was the only one who suffered." As the loud-speaker announced the departure of a flight from the gate next to them, he put his finger under her chin to gently raise her face, then lowered his mouth to hers.

His touch was so gentle and tender and held such a taste of love that Tracy's heart raced. She clung to him tightly, wishing that the kiss would never end, for she could live and die in the promises that it held.

When the noises of the airport finally penetrated, Josh pulled away slightly, but his eyes never left her for long. He picked up his briefcase, put his arm around her, and they walked toward the main terminal to collect his baggage.

"You know, I did a lot of thinking while I was gone," he told her quietly. A young couple, weaving in and out of the crowd, raced past them. "I hated being away from you, but it forced me to take a look at things."

Tracy didn't know what he was getting at, but with his arm so safely around her, she wasn't afraid.

"I realized I'd been so stupid about a lot of things," he went on, stopping to brush the top of her hair with his lips. "I was so sure that I couldn't trust a woman again that I didn't pause to realize how much you trusted me. Look at all those stupid rules that I set up. I was thinking about everything while I was in Washington and wondered why in the world you agreed to them."

"And what answer did you come up with?" she asked.

Josh looked around, noticing three men in uniform watching Tracy with all too apparent interest, and pulled her off to the side of the hallway. A huge lighted sign advertising *Time* magazine dwarfed them.

"I decided you cared about me enough to put up with my stupidity," he said. "And that I cared enough about you to know what was really important."

"And what's that?" she whispered, her eyes searching his face for a clue.

"That we're perfect for each other and belong together," he said simply. "I want to marry you, Tracy, if you'll have me."

Tracy could not believe her ears at first, then flew into action, throwing her arms around his neck. "Oh, Josh! Are you finally sure?" she cried happily. "Can you really love me as much as I love you?"

He kissed her soundly, then grinned down at her. "Actually, I decided it would be cheaper than having to hire you each time I need a fiancée."

She smiled back. "Always the romantic, aren't you?"

"As evidenced by the romantic setting I chose," he laughed. "Come on, let's get my suitcase and go back to your place, where we can celebrate properly."

She nodded and moved back into the security of his arm. They had more to celebrate than he knew now, she thought with a secret smile. How foolish she had been to worry! Everything was going to be fine!

* * *

"My God, you're beautiful," Josh sighed as his right hand roamed lightly over her body. He was lying on his left side next to her, his head supported in his hand, looking down at her. "I never thought I'd find someone as perfect for me as you are."

Tracy smiled up at him. Her eyes were darkened with passion as his hand softly caressed first one breast, then the other. When he bent his head to tease the dark pink tips with his mouth, she reached up her hands, sliding them through his thick hair with pleasure. His skin was slightly sweaty and her fingers, moving to his broad shoulders and back, slid across it smoothly. The rough hair that covered his body only added to the tantalizing thrill of touching him.

After making her body tingle and hunger for his touch, his lips left her breasts to search along her neck and around her ears for more fields to conquer. He found one particularly sensitive spot, and she quivered and moaned with desire.

Everything he did felt so good, better than ever before, and she wondered if it was knowing that her love was returned that did it; or could pregnancy have heightened her desires?

Rapidly losing herself to the pleasure his hands were giving, she tried to give him equal satisfaction. Her hands moved blindly over him, touching and caressing until neither could speak, their bodies and souls merged into a timeless burst of ecstasy.

As their hearts began to beat more normally, Tracy snuggled up to Josh. He was lying on his back next to her. "I have the most wonderful surprise for you," she whispered softly, not wanting to hold back her news any longer.

He opened one eye. "Dinner?" he asked hopefully.

She gave him a playful punch in the ribs, then took his hand between hers and kissed it. "Josh, I'm pregnant," she told him quietly.

Beyond stiffening slightly he seemed to have no reaction. "You're what?" he repeated, pulling his hand from hers to sit up.

She smiled and sat up too. "That was my reaction," she laughed. "But it's true. The doctor said my chances of getting pregnant were really small, but apparently our timing was perfect."

"Our timing?" he questioned in a deathly still voice.

She sensed him withdrawing further from her, and her stomach tightened in fear. "Well, I didn't get pregnant alone," she reminded him. Her smile no longer touched her eyes, which reflected her uncertainty.

"No, I never imagined you did," Josh agreed. He swung himself off the bed and reached for his clothes. "I don't know why you think I should be delighted with your news, though. Certainly the child's father would be the one to share it with." His back to her, he pulled his jeans on and zipped them up.

"But you are the father!" Tracy cried. Never in all her worrying had she dreamed that he would doubt it was his child. "There hasn't been anyone else."

He turned to face her as he put his shirt on, buttoning the buttons quickly. "Maybe not since Christmas," he shrugged coldly. "What happened? Did he dump you when he found out the happy news? I really played into your hands then, didn't I? Some other chump to lay the blame on; except I'm not so stupid as you think."

Sitting on the edge of the bed, he pulled his socks on, as Tracy threw her robe around her. "Josh, why are you doing this?" she pleaded with him, moving next to him. He spotted his shoes and went to get them, ignoring her. "You have to answer me," she screamed after him.

He stopped and turned to look at her coldly. It was the old Josh, the one no one could get close to, not the man she had been loving for the last two months. "I know it's not my child, simply because I cannot father one," he stated baldly. "I had the mumps as a teenager and I am sterile."

She just shook her head at his words. "But you're not," she insisted. "If you were sterile I wouldn't be pregnant."

Giving her a wry look, he turned to put his shoes on. "Give it up, Tracy; you can't win. This isn't just a vague idea I have. It's a fact. Confirmed by a doctor and grounds for divorce."

"That's why she divorced you?" Tracy whispered.

"Why not?" he shrugged. "She didn't want half a man."

His words echoed thoughts she had had about herself in the past and suddenly the pieces began to fall into place with painful accuracy. "Now I understand," she murmured to herself. Josh turned to stare at her, for her voice had lost that bewildered sound, leaving it brittle and emotionless.

"It all started when you found out that I

couldn't have kids, or thought I couldn't," she said. Her eyes were hard to cover the unbearable ache. "Suddenly I was safe. Since I was 'half a woman,' I could hardly demand a 'real' man. In fact, I probably would never even know, right? You wouldn't have told me, would you?"

"I don't know," he admitted harshly. "Maybe not."

Tracy closed her eyes briefly. He had chosen the wrong item to argue and so had proven that she had not lost anything, because there never was anything there to lose. When her eyes opened again, they were blazing with anger, but her voice was quiet and controlled. "I am not half a woman," she said. "Even if it were true and I couldn't have a child, I still would not be half a woman."

"That's not the point," he frowned.

"Oh, yes it is," she cried, no longer bothering to control herself. "It's the whole point. I suffered terribly when I thought I couldn't have a child. I was sure I was worthless and that David was right to leave. It took me a long time, but I finally came to see that that didn't matter to who I am and the kind of person I am. I am not more or less than any other woman just because of that little bit of scar tissue and it should not be the reason that anyone loves me or hates me."

"Who said it was?" he asked impatiently.

"Wasn't that my main attraction for you? Wasn't that behind all these little 'perfectly matched' remarks of yours?" She was pacing back and forth at the end of the bed, trying to find a way through the maze of pain. "I loved you. Isn't that a laugh?" She stopped walking and turned to glare at him. "And I thought you loved me, but just couldn't say it yet."

"What we thought we felt for each other is hardly the issue," he snapped. "It's a convenient way to distract me, but it won't work. I am not the father of your child."

"No, you're not," she said suddenly, her head held high. "He was someone kind and gentle and caring and I loved him deeply. The fact that the person I thought he was never really existed cannot change my love and it never will." She took a deep breath. "I think you had better go, Josh," she added quietly.

Words were unnecessary, for his eyes stared at her with hatred and the pain of betrayal. Then he turned and was gone. She did not move until she heard the door slam behind him, and then she slowly sank to the floor to cry for the death of her dreams.

Chapter Ten

TRACY'S MORNING SICKNESS returned, but refused to be relegated to just the mornings. None of the various diets Dr. Myers recommended seemed to have any effect, which surprised him but not her. All she had to do was think of Josh and she felt horrible. Seeing him was enough to ruin her appetite for days. She doubted there was any pill that cured heartache.

How could he have doubted her? she asked herself over and over again, her anger blazing anew each time she thought about him. Or had he? There was no way that she could check his convenient alibi. Maybe he had done what she had feared: decided that he wanted no part of her or the baby and left.

With these thoughts constantly in her mind, it was no wonder that her anger refused to die. February drifted into March, but time brought no soothing relief. The pain was always there.

She was excited, in a way, about the baby and looked forward to its arrival. The chance to be a mother was such an unexpected gift that she treasured it doubly, and tried to rid herself of the nagging feeling that she was being cheated. It should be a happy time, because this pregnancy was such a miracle, but Josh had stolen her peace of mind.

So many problems loomed ahead of her and she would have to face them alone.

In the first few despairing days after Josh's rejection of her, she had wondered if she should go ahead with the pregnancy. After all, Josh didn't want her or the baby, so why should she cling to a reminder of him? But she realized almost immediately that she could never have an abortion. She could not revenge her anger at Josh on his child, and besides, the baby was not just a souvenir of their affair to be discarded when love was gone. It was a part of her, and she would love and cherish it.

Her feelings toward Josh were much harder to analyze. She tried to convince herself that she no longer felt anything for him and that she'd like nothing better than to have him return so she could throw him out. But she doubted that it was that simple. She was angry now, but when that died away, she had no idea what she would discover.

Work was another problem. She would have liked to hide her condition as long as possible, or at least until she had things sorted out in her mind, but, as fate would have it, that was not to be.

One evening in the middle of March, most of the staff had to work late to cover the story of a man who had taken eight people hostage in a suburban restaurant. There really was little to do most of the time, just sit and wait, but Tracy was lucky enough to be sent out on another assignment.

The police were raiding an electronic-games parlor because citizens in the area had complained about young boys involved in homosexual prostitution. The place was quite crowded, and a number of arrests were made. Tracy got some great pictures in spite of the reluctance of some of the adult patrons to be photographed. Once back at the paper, she developed the prints carefully and was pleased with the results.

Josh had not been at the paper for the last few days. Apparently he had had to go back to Washington to do some more research on James Carlton, the real-estate developer who had been discovered to have been buying up large parcels of land on Chicago's west side. It was a relief to know that she would not run into him unexpectedly, and for the first time in weeks, she was able to relax.

After delivering her prints to layout, she went back to the picture desk. Maybe they could spare her for a half hour so that she could go out and get herself something to eat. Something plain like soup perhaps, for even though she was hungry, her stomach wasn't feeling too adventurous.

"Hi, Tracy, back already?" Bob Bineski asked when she came over to their end of the city room. "Hungry?"

He nodded to the half-eaten pizza that lay on Al's desk. Al was searching through a file cabinet, but looked up when she came in.

"Sure, help yourself. It's got everything," he told her.

The smells as she approached had told her that, for the minute she had come near, her stomach had begun to churn. Sausage, cheese, mushrooms, anchovies, and green peppers were not what she had a taste for just yet. The room suddenly swam before her eyes.

Oh, Lord, she thought, and raced toward the women's lounge down the hall. She was more than a little embarrassed when she returned.

"You okay?" Al asked with concern.

She nodded and sank into a chair, still feeling rather wobbly. The pizza, thank God, had disappeared.

"Maybe you're getting the flu," Bob suggested.

Tracy lifted her chin. Her jeans were getting too tight anyway, so there seemed little point in lying. They'd know soon enough. "If I do, it's the nine-month variety," she said.

Bob stared and Al coughed with embarrassment. "Uh, hey, Tracy, that's . . ." Al's voice died away.

Tracy's mouth curved into a reluctant smile at their uncertainty. Not really knowing her, they had no idea how she wanted them to react.

"Yeah, I was surprised, too," she told them.

"I didn't even know you had somebody," Al said, then shook his head with a frown. "I mean, looking at you, I should have known there'd be men around, but . . ."

Tracy patted his arm. "It's okay, I don't say much about the men I date."

"Are you getting married?" Bob asked. He was in his sixties and had been married for decades to the same woman. The idea of babies without wedding rings was apparently abhorrent.

She shook her head with an apologetic glance, knowing her answer would make him uncomfortable. "No, I'm afraid he hadn't had a long-term relationship in mind." Wanting to clarify things a little more, she added, "What I thought were emotional hangups from a previous marriage were only excuses to buy him time. I fear I was a bit of a fool."

"What are you going to do?" Al asked gently.

174

The concern in his eyes made her feel like crying. If only Josh had looked like that when she had told him . . .

"What is there to do?" she shrugged. "I won't have an abortion. I just couldn't. So that doesn't leave many alternatives. I suppose I could put the baby up for adoption, but I won't. I'll keep him, or her, and bore you all to death with pictures." She ended with a rather defiant laugh, as if she expected them to challenge her.

"Hey, if there's anything we can do, just tell us," Al said quietly.

Tears came to Tracy's eyes at their consideration. "Thank you," she whispered. "You've been really great."

"Yeah, we already dumped the pizza," Al added, trying to lighten the mood.

"But have you eaten?" Bob asked, not distracted by her words. "How about if I get you some chicken soup?" As he spoke, he reached into his pocket for some change.

The soup from the coffee machine was hardly gourmet fare, but it probably would stay in her stomach. "Yeah, I would like that," she said with a nod.

"I've got some crackers in my desk," Al offered, not to be outdone.

This was getting to be a little much and she frowned. "I'm not an invalid, you know. I don't need to be waited on."

"For today, let us wait on you," Al told her. "You know us newspapermen: we're fickle. By morning, we'll have another story and will forget you."

Tracy smiled slightly. "Okay," she said. "But tomorrow I'm pulling my weight around here."

Tomorrow was not quite a different story. No one offered to buy her chicken soup or gave her the crackers he had stored in his desk, but she had not returned to the ranks of "one of the guys."

The assignments she got were given carefully—nothing that might be too strenuous or dangerous. City-hall duty was hers, and she got to photograph the thirteen-year-old who saved his older brother's life by rushing him to the hospital. Then one of Chicago's few sets of quadruplets had their fourth birthday, and she was there.

As much as she appreciated everyone's concern, things were getting boring, and Tracy prayed that soon they would forget she was pregnant. She could not take another six months of such assignments.

"I need a photographer," Josh told Al one morning a few days later. Although he tried not to let them, his eyes strayed over to where Tracy was going over a schedule. She looked exhausted, and his heart went out to her. In spite of her lies and attempt to trick him, he still cared what happened to her.

"Reilly's in the darkroom, but he should be free soon," Al told him.

Josh's eyes went back to Tracy with a frown. "What about Tracy?" he asked.

Al glanced her way, but apparently she had not heard them. He gestured for Josh to come over to the coffee machine at the end of the city room with him.

"I'm not sending Tracy out on a lot of assignments," Al confided to Josh as he put his quarter into the machine and pressed the button for black coffee. He watched it run into his cup; by the time he could get it, they were alone.

"Why not?"

Al glanced around again, then leaned closer to Josh, confidentially. "Some bastard got her pregnant, then took a walk," he told him, not noticing Josh's sudden stiffening. "She wants to have the baby, though God knows why," he added with a bewildered shake of the head. "She ought to just get rid of the thing and forget about him, but she's not. Going to raise the kid herself." He shook his head again. "Anyway, she's been feeling pretty shaky, so I'm trying not to give her too much to do. You understand," he added, looking questioningly up at Josh.

Nodding, Josh got himself a cup of coffee to hide his own feelings. So Tracy had not told anyone who the father of her child was. Since the guy wasn't around anymore that wasn't surprising, but Josh had half expected her to try to implicate *him*. And how easy that would have been if he had not insisted all along that they keep their relationship quiet.

Al went back to his desk, but Josh leaned against a nearby file cabinet, staring down the hallway. He had really fallen into her trap, he thought. He had believed all that nonsense about not being able to get pregnant and had felt safe with her. Safe! What a joke! He threw away his half-empty coffee cup with disgust.

The way she had all the people at work pampering her was proof enough of her connivance.

She was out to get her own way and didn't care whom she hurt in the process.

He turned around suddenly and was startled to find Tracy at the coffee machine. She stopped, equally surprised to find him standing there, glaring at her.

"Hello, Josh," she said quietly. "How are you?"

"I don't need to ask *you* that," he snapped, irritated with her courageous-victim act. "I see you've got everybody here looking out for you. You must play the role of the injured party quite well."

She blinked, but did not answer. Her eyes looked hurt and tired. The bouncy vitality that had been so much a part of her seemed gone. Josh turned away suddenly, fighting the powerful urge to take her in his arms. Realizing his desire made him furious. She was the one who had betrayed his trust, his concern, and he was the one who had been played for a fool. How could he still want her and care about her?

Matt Reilly came out into the city room, his camera case swung over his shoulder.

"It's about time you're ready," Josh barked, finding a convenient target for his anger. "What'd you think? The fire was going to wait for you to get there before burning out?"

Tracy waited until Josh was out of sight, pretending to be studying the selections available in the coffee machine. Then she turned and walked slowly back to the picture desk. The cup of hot chocolate she had been going to get was forgotten.

Until Josh had walked into the office a few minutes earlier, she hadn't known that he was back, and his appearance had shaken her more than she would have thought possible. In the several days since she had seen him last, she had felt some of her anger and despair melting away, and life had begun to fall into a routine again. Stupidly, she had supposed that she would be immune to his presence once he returned.

What a laugh! she thought bitterly. Even though he clearly could not stand the sight of her, nothing much had changed for her. Without the protective shell of her anger, she still ached and longed for him and the security of his love. She was so exhausted and wanted nothing more than to rest in his arms and have him soothe away her hurts.

"Oh, there you are, Tracy." Al looked up from his desk. "A Paul Hanson from the legal department just called. Wanted to see you in his office as soon as possible."

Tracy frowned. "What about?"

"Who knows?" Al shrugged. "But he didn't sound as if he was about to fire you." He turned to go back to his desk. "We can spare you now, if you want to see what it's all about."

"Okay," Tracy agreed and turned back toward the elevator. It certainly was true that they could spare her. She didn't do much lately except take up space and, now, sort out negatives from their files outside the darkroom. Somehow their files had gotten messed up and Al had asked her to try to get them back in order. Actually, she wouldn't have been surprised to learn that Al had messed them up himself in order to keep her from going out on too many assignments.

The legal offices looked as if they were in a different building, not just on a different floor. There were rugs on the floor, and the walls were paneled in rich wood, not some cheap laminated stuff. Huge plants resided in corners, mysteriously flourishing without lights, and the secretaries talked in whispers. Unfortunately, all the elegant surroundings could not take the smell of the ink from the air.

Paul Hanson was not high on the seniority list, and his office was down a narrow hallway from the elevator. His plants did not look as if they had just stepped out of the jungle, and his secretary had a rasping cough. Tracy was treated with great courtesy, however, which she noted silently: apparently she was not in hot water about anything.

"Miss Monroe." A tall, thin man in his late thirties had come out of the office to greet her. His gray pinstripe suit was immaculate and superbly offset by his white shirt and deep red tie. The thin metal frames of his glasses added a touch of seriousness to his demeanor, which was a little too perfect to feel comfortable with. Tracy greeted him cautiously.

"Come into my office," he invited her graciously. "Would you like some coffee?"

"No, thank you," Tracy replied rather automatically, glancing around his office. It was not particularly spacious, but the furnishings were expensive, if a little shabby.

Mr. Hanson waved her to the caramel-colored leather sofa along one wall. She skirted the table before it, and sat down. He took the adjacent chair, a confidential smile on his face that Tracy did not trust one inch.

"I must commend you for your promptness," he said smoothly. "Although there was no hurry."

Tracy said nothing, just watching him closely. She hadn't a clue as to what this was all about, but something smelled decidedly fishy. Her face gave none of her thoughts away.

He shifted his position slightly so that he was leaning forward. "Actually, it's about some pictures you took the other day," he began. "At an electronic-games parlor."

He paused expectantly and Tracy nodded.

"Well, one of the policemen working on the case had seen some of the pictures in the paper and called me. He wondered if he could get a copy of your pictures for his investigation."

"Certainly," Tracy responded calmly. She wondered why a routine request was being handled in such a strange way, but kept her voice carefully controlled. "I've provided the police with prints before. Just give me his name and I'll get what he wants to him."

Mr. Hanson coughed slightly and leaned back. "I'm afraid he asked for the pictures in confidence," he explained hesitantly.

Curiouser and curiouser, Tracy thought, though she nodded again. "I see. Then he told you what he wants?"

The lawyer nodded with a smile. He seemed to be relieved at her apparent agreement. "It's a matter of police security, you see," he told her patronizingly. "He needs the prints and the negatives. For his case," he added quickly.

Tracy just looked at him, her curiosity aroused by his obviously false story. No policeman would ask for her negatives, and certainly not through someone else. They occasionally asked for prints, and once in a great while asked to borrow a nega-

181

tive, but they always came to the photographer directly. The problem was, who really wanted them, and how much did this lawyer know?

"We don't usually give out the negatives," she said slowly. "It's not our policy."

Mr. Hanson was not pleased with her response and frowned severely. Unfortunately, it did not intimidate her as intended. "I had assured the police that we'd be cooperative," he told her, the charm gone from his voice. "That they would not need a court order."

"Goodness, I hadn't realized it was that serious," she murmured with mock contrition in her voice.

Mr. Hanson continued to look stern and forbidding but Tracy could see his eyes relax. It was obvious that he thought she had bought his weird little story. "Then you'll get the prints and negatives to me?" he asked her, then glanced at his watch. "It's late, I realize, but they did want them today and it shouldn't take you long to gather the things together. In fact," he unbent slightly to graciousness, "I'll send Miss D'Alessandro down with you and save you the trip back up."

My, my, he was in a hurry, Tracy noted with interest. Next he'd be offering to come down himself. "I'm afraid it's not quite as simple as pulling the things from a drawer," she told him with an apologetic smile. "We had a little mishap with our negatives. Someone got into them and they're a real mess—" Her voice trailed off suddenly as she wondered if there was any connection. Maybe it had nothing to do with Al.

Mr. Hanson's eyes narrowed suspiciously at her abrupt silence, and Tracy's nerves jangled a warning as this whole incident took on slightly more serious proportions. "Actually," she jumped into speech quickly with her most vacuous smile, quickly inventing an employee to blame. "We've got this new kid helping out and he's impossible. The place is such a mess, but he's somebody's nephew and we're stuck with him. He'd normally be the one to find the prints for you, but that would take days," she said with a flash of inspiration. "But I promise to look for them myself and try to get them to you by tomorrow or the day after."

"Well, if that's the soonest you can get them," he sighed, and rose to his feet. "You've been very cooperative."

Tracy just continued to smile and tried to look impressed with him and his office as she went toward the door. She could hardly wait to get her hands on those negatives and find out who was in those pictures. It was obviously someone who didn't want to be seen.

Al agreed with her. "It sounds like one terrific story," he said, his eyes lighting up with interest. "You find those negatives; I'll see if I can get a reporter to help you do some digging."

He hurried across the room to talk to the city editor while she went across the hall to tackle the pile of negatives, more certain than ever that someone had tried to find the shots on their own and only tried this new angle when they had failed.

"Great news," Al came over to tell her. "The city editor was really interested in the story, too, and gave us one of his top reporters to work with you."

"Oh?" Tracy had found some pictures she had taken the day before the ones she wanted. Maybe she was getting close. "Who's he going to send?"

"Rettinger."

Chapter Eleven

"WELL, WHERE ARE WE supposed to begin?" Josh asked Tracy impatiently as he sat down at the table where she was sorting negatives. They were in the small room outside the darkroom that the photographers used for storing equipment, so they had a little privacy for him to vent his anger. He hadn't been able to believe it when he had returned from covering that arson on Roosevelt Road and had been told he was working on a special case with Tracy. How the hell had she arranged that? And what did she hope to gain by it?

Tracy glanced up at him briefly and then continued with her work. "I hadn't expected you'd want to start until tomorrow," she said simply. "This story is hardly the most exciting way to spend an evening."

Her words were innocently said but they brought back a strong reminder of how happily his evenings had been spent a few weeks ago, and along with that memory came the pain. "Actually, my friend was most understanding when I explained that I had to work late and made me promise that I'd come to her place as soon as I left here," he said smoothly.

Tracy did not look up, but her knuckles whitened as she clutched some negatives. "Well, you needn't stay if you don't want to," she told him quietly, with a slight quiver in her voice. "I have to make prints of all the shots I took, and then enlarge some of them. There really isn't any need for you to wait around while I do that."

Tracy looked at him as she finished speaking; when Josh saw how white her face was, he was ashamed of himself. "I didn't have a date," he admitted impatiently, but whether the cause of his irritation was himself or her, he did not know and did not care to analyze.

She sighed and laid down the negatives in her hand as she leaned back in her chair. "This isn't going to work, you know that," she told him. "There isn't any way that we can work together."

"I don't see any way we can avoid it, either," he snapped. "I'm not about to start looking for a different job, and I know you won't either. After all, maternity benefits don't start immediately, do they?"

He saw the look of anguish flash across her face before she turned away. Damnit, he cursed himself, why couldn't he keep his mouth shut?

He knew that she deserved everything he said and more, for hadn't she tried to trap him with her lies? But it didn't help to know that. As much as he wanted to strike out at her and hurt her the way she had hurt him, the desire to hold her and love her was far stronger. He jumped to his feet in an effort to save his sanity.

"I need a cup of coffee," he announced, as if this excused his despicable behavior. "Can I get you one?"

Tracy shook her head. "No, thanks," she said, her voice little more than a harsh whisper. After she cleared her throat, it became stronger. "Coffee hasn't been agreeing with me lately."

He nodded and left the room. He had to get hold of himself, he thought sternly as he walked across the hall to the city room. He had to prove that she no longer had any attraction for him, that he did not care about her anymore. Once this assignment was over, he would be able to relax, for no other could be as hard. He would have survived the test. He could work with her again and think nothing of it.

Slamming his quarter into the coffee machine, Josh punched the button for black coffee and watched as it drained into the cup below. Who was he kidding? It was going to be hell to get Tracy out of his system. A thousand times as hard as it had been to forget Monica.

Tracy had seemed so right for him, so perfect. And it wasn't just that he had thought that she would not be condemning of his inability to father a child, it was so much more. Everything about her seemed to blend with and balance him. She made him feel alive as he never had before; even learning that she had lied had not killed his feelings for her. His feelings were wounded, certainly, but still there, leaping to life at the sight of her.

Tossing away his half-finished coffee, he trudged back across the hall. Maybe he could learn to get used to her presence, and in time would forget the few weeks of happiness they had shared. But, for now, he would keep his emotions in check and treat her as if she were a stranger.

Tracy looked up when he entered the room. Her eyes were reddened slightly as if she had been crying, but he forced himself not to think about it.

"Al filled me in on most of the details," he said quite matter-of-factly. "I thought the first thing I should do is check with the police in charge of the case to make certain that they hadn't actually asked for the pictures."

She nodded toward a phone on the far wall. "I'll get started developing the pictures then, while you do that," she offered, echoing his businesslike manner.

Josh watched as she disappeared into the darkroom and the light flashed on, a warning for no one to enter. There was no way around it: this assignment was going to be hell. He went over to the phone and picked it up. Maybe he could get the story wrapped up quickly.

When the warning light went out over the darkroom door a little later, Josh knocked. "Can I come in now?" he asked.

Tracy pushed the door open and he slipped inside. She was working at a counter across the small room from the door. "Close the door all the way," she warned as she flicked the switch to turn the outside warning light back on. At the same time, the red safelight went on inside the darkroom, covering everything with an eerie red glow.

"Did you reach the police?" she asked as she adjusted the enlarger and slipped a piece of printing paper underneath it. She turned a switch and a light went on, turning off automatically after twenty seconds.

Josh leaned up against the door, watching her work. Her body moved gracefully, with no wasted actions, as she dipped the paper into the developing fluid, moving it around in the pan with a pair of print tongs. Desire burned deep within him, even as she turned slightly and he could see her thickening waist. If only that were his child growing inside her . . .

Tracy turned suddenly. "Did you call the police or not?" she repeated, with a hint of impatience in her voice.

Josh started. "Uh, yeah, but I couldn't reach the officer in charge of the investigation. He's off duty now, but I did talk to one of the men that worked on it," he said quickly. Forcing his eyes away from Tracy's body, he took a few steps across the room to look at some of the pictures she had already developed.

She had taken a print out of the first of several pans and slipped it into the stop bath, when she noticed Josh studying one of the finished prints. "Recognize anybody?"

He shook his head and looked up. "I spoke to an Officer Hailey, who knew of no request to get the prints. Couldn't figure out what they'd do with them if they did get them," Josh said and shrugged. "Apparently they had had a lot of complaints about that parlor from the neighborhood and had raided it more for publicity value than to make any lasting arrests. So having the pictures wouldn't matter to them. It sounds to me like someone in the pictures is afraid he's going to get recognized, and wants them destroyed."

"That's what I thought," Tracy agreed absently as she continued to print pictures and move them along the assembly line of developing pans.

Josh tried to concentrate on the photographs, searching for some face that might look familiar or more worried than the others, but it was impossible. His eyes kept straying to her hands as they moved so confidently about her work. Each movement she made in developing the pictures reminded him of times they had been together, when her hands had caressed him and slid across his body as firmly and surely as they moved across the enlarger.

"I thought that picture was the best," Tracy said, breaking the spell of his thoughts and nodding toward the last picture she had developed. "It shows just about all the people who are in the other shots, so I thought I'd enlarge it section by section, and we'd get a better look at everybody in the background there."

"Sounds good," he agreed, more aware of her presence as she moved over to explain than what she was actually saying.

"If I zero in on these people along here and adjust the exposure time," she went on, "we ought to be able to get a clearer picture of all these people in the shadows."

As she reached in front of him to show what she meant, Josh moved slightly and their bodies accidentally touched. A current of desire raced through him, sudden and devastatingly strong. She turned, as if drawn by the same flame, and suddenly she was in his arms.

"Oh, Tracy," Josh moaned softly as he pulled her closer to him, his mouth devouring hers with an insatiable hunger. It had been so long since he had held her that she was all he could think of. Her soft body beneath his. Her hands, small, but wielding so much power over him. Her lips, soft and moist and eager.

His hands roamed over her back, unable to stop

their caress as his tongue plundered her mouth. He needed her so. She was such a part of him.

Tormented by the ecstasy of his embrace, Tracy wished that time would stand still. Just a few minutes ago she had been in such pain, fearing what the immediate future would hold. All she had was this moment; and even now she could feel Josh slipping away from her.

Suddenly she was out of his arms, and he had spun around. His back was to her and he leaned heavily against the counter. "Damn!" he muttered.

Taking a small step toward him, Tracy reached out and touched his arm lightly. She felt him stiffen, but he did not pull away.

"Josh," she said softly. "Can we talk?"

He turned around to look at her, his face expressionless and cold. She hated it when he got like that for she felt there was no way to break through the wall he built around himself. She'd rather face his anger than such apparent indifference.

"What is there to talk about?" he asked curtly. "So I'm attracted to you physically; that doesn't really mean anything, you know."

She tried to ignore his hateful words because she didn't really think he meant them. "Don't do this to us," she pleaded. "Don't keep pushing me away."

His eyes froze up even more. "There is no us," he said. "Or are you going to tell me that you aren't really pregnant?"

She sighed at his stubborn immobility. "Josh,

please listen to me for a moment. Without all your anger and hatred.''

For a second, his eyes reflected the agony in his heart. ''I don't hate you,'' he whispered. ''I wish to God I could.''

It hardly was a positive response, but Tracy went on. ''Josh, I was not lying to you when I told you this was your child. There has been no other man since my divorce.''

He snorted with disbelief. ''Yes, I dated some,'' she admitted quickly. ''But I never slept with any of them. I never wanted to. Not until I met you.''

''What's the point of all this? Is my love for you supposed to be so strong that I'll believe my doctor was wrong and you're right?'' he sneered, looking away with impatience.

''Yes.''

He turned to stare at her in complete astonishment and she gazed back, her heart in her eyes. ''Then it's too bad that there is no love,'' he said harshly.

She felt cut and bleeding from his cruelty, but forced herself to go on. ''That doesn't matter,'' she insisted sadly. ''I'm not fighting for myself anymore. I'm a big girl and knew what I was getting into. I don't expect you to marry me. But your child has a right to know its father and you have a right to know that you have a child, whether you want it or not.''

''How very unselfish of you,'' he jeered. ''Unfortunately, it doesn't change the facts. What do you need, a note from my doctor?''

''Yes,'' she answered quickly, her voice desperately eager. ''Go see your doctor again. If he says you can't be the father of my child, I won't bother you again. I'll even get a different job if you want."

He could not believe what she was saying. "These conditions don't change," he told her.

"Of course they can," she argued, suddenly hopeful. "It's been ten years since your divorce. A lot could have happened." She thought for a moment that he was really listening, so she went on. "Josh, what if I'm right and this is your child? Can you turn your back on it out of sheer stubbornness?"

"You're the one being stubborn, not I," he said curtly, his forbidding glare back in place. "You're reaching for straws that just aren't there." He turned and without warning left the room.

"Josh!" Tracy cried, in agony and anger. Not only had he walked out unconvinced by her arguments, but he had let the light in, ruining most of her pictures.

Tracy had all the pictures and enlargements finished by the time Josh came around in the morning. She had had little sleep the night before, but a careful application of makeup hid the signs. Yet as long as the night had been, she felt she had accomplished something. She had finally come to see that Josh was not going to change his mind. Working with him would be an agony, but she would do it. She was going to ignore his insults and gibes and be businesslike and controlled. No subject unrelated to their jobs would be brought up by her, and if he brought one up, she would ignore it. She had faced reality last night and come to grips with it.

"Good morning," she greeted Josh coolly

when he came into the room. Bob was working in the files, but his presence made no difference. Josh was just another reporter she worked with, and she would treat him just the same. "I've got the pictures laid out here," she told him, indicating the worktable in the corner.

Josh said nothing as he walked over to the table, and Tracy was careful not to look at him except for quick glances now and then. She didn't care what he thought or how he looked. She was through caring.

"I got ahold of that police officer," he told her, looking down at the pictures. "He had never even heard of Hanson, let alone asked him for some pictures. He agreed that the whole thing sounded pretty fishy, but that so far it didn't seem that anyone had broken the law—just lied a bit."

Tracy nodded, and spread her pictures out. "We've all looked at them and don't recognize a soul," she told him.

Josh picked up her enlargements one by one, studying each carefully. "I sure don't recognize anyone either," he admitted after a few moments. "Did you decide who looked the guiltiest?"

"Yeah, all of them over thirty," Bob cracked.

Tracy let a small smile form on her lips. "Actually, there are three people who looked rather uncomfortable." She picked up a pen and pulled two enlargements over. "These two men in suits," she said, pointing out two men next to each other in one picture. She turned to the other picture. "And this guy with the white streak in his hair."

Josh looked closely at him. "With that hair, he certainly shows up even in the smaller pictures."

"Might be a reason to be scared," she agreed.

"But we have no proof and, even if we did, who cares that some guy with a white streak in his hair prefers boys to girls?"

"If that's all there was to it, yeah." Josh pulled a chair out and sat down. He looked through the pictures again as he talked. "But you're forgetting the lawyer upstairs. How is it he's willing to lie for this other guy?"

Tracy sat down with a tired sigh, the sleepless night suddenly catching up with her. "Yeah, you're right," she agreed listlessly. Maybe she should have forced herself to eat something for breakfast after all.

"Hey, are you okay?" Josh asked.

Tracy had been staring ahead of her, but looked up at him with a forced smile on her face. "Sure, I was just trying to think where we go from here," she said briskly, then picked up some pictures to pretend to study. She was not going to make that same mistake of seeing concern in his eyes where there was none.

"I don't think you go anywhere from here, unless it's home to get some rest. You look awful," he announced dictatorially. She glared at him, but he continued, "I'm going to do some looking into our Mr. Hanson." He picked up a couple of pictures as he stood up. "Might as well take a few of these along," he noted and, after a quick nod to Bob, he walked toward the door.

"I assume you'll let me know what you find out," she called sarcastically after him.

"If you need to know," he tossed out as he left.

"Damn, arrogant jerk," Tracy muttered while she gathered up her pictures. "Why did he have to be assigned to work with me?"

Bob looked up from his work. "He'll do a good job," he pointed out, as his phone began to ring.

"If that's Al with an assignment, I'm taking it," Tracy informed Bob as he reached for the phone. Keeping busy seemed to be the only way to keep Josh out of her mind.

It took Josh only a few phone calls to learn that Paul Hanson was a man who lived considerably beyond his means. The Cook County Credit Bureau had quite a list of companies to which he owed money, from the American National Bank to a small local department store. Several of those companies readily admitted that he was deeply in debt and falling further behind all the time. From a street connection, Josh also learned that a loan shark had his hooks into Hanson and that Hanson was getting desperate for money. It wasn't too hard to figure out just what had happened: Someone had offered him some money for the pictures, and he'd agreed. A talk with Mr. Hanson might very well clear up the whole problem; Josh dialed his number. Unfortunately, he was not in his office at the time, so Josh made an appointment for later in the day.

As he hung up his phone, Josh did not know whether to be happy that this assignment was settling so quickly, or sad. True, it was difficult working with Tracy, but it was an excuse to see her; and he knew that he needed that. As much as he tried, he could not keep her out of his mind.

She had looked awful this morning, as if she hadn't eaten or slept for days. He knew that pregnancy was hard on some women; but was that all, or was he partly to blame?

Moving suddenly, he went over to some shelves near the file cabinets at one end of the room and got a phone book to take back to his desk. He found the section that listed doctors. It wouldn't hurt to call and ask, he told himself.

The first urologist he called was not in, and the next was unavailable at the moment. But at the third, after identifying himself as a reporter trying to verify some information, a Dr. Halvaseck came to the phone.

"We're doing a story on infertility," Josh lied glibly. "And I'm afraid the person doing the research left out a few points." He took a deep breath, wondering if he really wanted to know. "Can a man whose sterility was caused by a case of the mumps become fertile again?"

"Well," the doctor said. "There are a number of things that can cause temporary sterility in a man as well as a woman, but when the reproductive organs themselves are damaged severely, the body cannot correct the problem. We can fix some things with surgery, but that's not one of them."

"So the answer is no?" Josh asked, wanting things in plain English.

"The answer is no," the doctor agreed.

Somehow, Josh managed to get off the phone coherently, then picked up his coat and left the office. What had he expected? he asked himself as he walked down Michigan Avenue. A freezing rain was falling but he did not notice.

He had known from the beginning that that child was not his, hadn't he? It didn't matter that Tracy had convinced him that there might be a chance. She was a good talker, that's all.

On the bridge, he stopped walking, leaned on

the railing, and looked down at the Chicago River. The problem was, he had wanted it to be his child. He had wanted Tracy to be telling him the truth because he loved her so. He had wanted to believe the impossible.

Closing his eyes, he remembered how Monica had sobbed when she told him of the doctor's report. He could never forget how devastated he had felt. By that time, Monica had not meant much to him—certainly not what Tracy meant to him—but he had shared her sorrow. She had wanted children, hoping that they would give the marriage meaning again, but he couldn't give them to her. He had not been able to do anything to make her happy. His job was in the wrong place, he didn't have a wide circle of partying friends, and he was unable to give her children. The only thing he could do was give her her freedom.

He had been so sure that things would be different with Tracy. She was so unselfish and caring and he knew she wouldn't care about his sterility. Or he thought he knew it. She had seemed so different from the other women he had known. And, despite her charge, he had planned to tell her. He wasn't going to keep it a secret, but he had been worried. Monica had divorced him because he couldn't have kids. He had been afraid that Tracy would not want him either—regardless of what she said was her own condition.

The rain began to penetrate his coat and Josh turned back the way he had come, passing the newspaper building and going on to Billy Goat's Tavern. There he had a long lunch, consisting of half a hamburger and several beers. By the time he returned to the office, he had convinced himself that he did not care about Tracy. All he needed was a new woman in his life; then he wouldn't even remember Tracy's name.

"There are some messages on your desk, Rettinger," the assistant editor called to him when he walked across the city room.

Josh waved in acknowledgment and picked up the pink message notes. Tracy had called. He tossed that into the wastebasket. Mr. Hanson's secretary had canceled his appointment for that afternoon, and one of his connections on the street had called about the building-code story he had been working on. Terribly exciting, Josh thought cynically as he sank into his chair and picked up the last message. Denise had called.

Staring at the paper for a long moment, Josh decided she was just what he needed. Just a little fun. He reached over to pick up his phone and dial the number on the message.

Chapter Twelve

"WHAT IN THE WORLD have you been doing to yourself?"

Tracy just shrugged and avoided Dr. Myers's eyes by letting her gaze stray to the pictures on the shelf behind his desk. "I haven't been able to eat much," she said.

"It's not just the lost weight, Tracy," he told her sternly. "Your blood pressure is up, too. You were in much better shape when you were in last month than you are now."

"Things haven't been going too well," she admitted quietly, remembering Josh's behavior when they worked together yesterday. "I've been eating what I can, but, well, it's been harder than I thought," she ended lamely.

The doctor leaned back in his chair and watched her for a moment. "Is it the boyfriend?" he asked gently.

Tracy looked over at him. "What boyfriend?" Her voice was cynical and hard.

"He did a disappearing act, I take it?"

She shook her head. "Unfortunately, he's only half gone," she said. "We still have to work together and pretend to be civil to each other. It's not particularly easy."

"Maybe you should find a different job," he

suggested. Tapping his fingers absently on the arm of his chair, he watched for her reaction.

Tracy stood up with a sigh and walked over to the window. She peeked through the blinds to watch the cars in the street below. The piles of snow on the edge of the sidewalk looked even filthier from up here. "I had considered it, but maternity benefits don't start immediately and I'm going to need all the help I can get." She turned around to face him. "I just can't afford to leave."

"Maybe you can't afford not to," he pointed out.

She frowned in confusion, then shook her head. "I'll get used to working with him," she insisted. "It'll take some time, but I'll get used to it."

"Tracy, you may not have a lot of time at your disposal," he told her, leaning forward again. "You're not taking care of yourself at a time when your body needs pampering. You need lots of nourishing foods and you are starving yourself. It's obvious that you aren't getting enough rest, and that blood pressure is terrible. If you don't want to lose the baby, you'd better make some drastic changes."

"Lose the baby?" Tracy echoed fearfully as she sank back into her chair. "You mean I might?"

He nodded, his face stern. "The rate you're going, I'd bet on it. The question is, is that what you want?"

Tracy was taken aback by his words, her eyes open wide with astonishment. "How can you ask if that's what I want?" she cried. "Of course I don't want to lose my baby! If I didn't want it, I would have had an abortion!"

"Maybe," he said cryptically. "Or maybe this

is your way of accomplishing that. Without any guilt to nag at you.''

Tracy just stared at him, totally bewildered that he could think such things.

''Or maybe what you really want is to punish your boyfriend. Lose the baby and place all the blame on him,'' the doctor went on coldly. ''That would serve him right for abandoning you.''

Shaking her head dumbly, tears came to her eyes. ''No,'' she whispered. ''You're wrong. This baby is very important to me. I don't want to lose it.''

''Then fight for it!'' he cried, waving his arms in exasperation. ''Get yourself a different job if that's necessary! Or else come to terms with yourself and your ex-boyfriend! Your baby's life is dependent on how well you can pull yourself together.''

''I will,'' she said quietly with a nod.

''The first thing you have to do is start eating,'' he went on. ''Fill your refrigerator with yogurt.''

She made a face. ''I hate it.''

He looked unimpressed. ''Learn to like it. It's one thing that will settle your stomach. Then I'd like you to get away for some rest. Do nothing but eat and sleep and lie around. For at least a week,'' he added.

''A week?''

He nodded. ''It'll give your body a chance to recuperate, and it'll give you a chance to decide if you can keep working with your ex-boyfriend.''

''All right,'' she agreed numbly. ''I think I can get some time off. I can't afford to go anywhere, but I promise to rest and do my thinking.'' She picked up her purse and stood up.

"Remember what's at stake," he added warningly as she left his office.

How could she forget? Tracy thought as she sat in a cab going the mile or so back to the newspaper. He had succeeded in scaring the hell out of her.

She was not going to lose her baby, she told herself, staring out the cab window. She wanted it very much, regardless of what the doctor had suggested. Josh had suddenly fallen very far back in her priorities. Nothing and no one was more important than her baby. To prove it, the first thing she was going to do was get some lunch.

The cab stopped in front of the newspaper and Tracy paid the driver and stepped onto the sidewalk. It was starting to snow, she realized with a shiver, glancing up at the leaden sky. Was this winter ever going to end?

Tracy had hoped to have a message from Josh when she returned from her doctor's appointment, for she wondered if he had learned anything about Mr. Hanson. She was determined to follow Dr. Myers's instructions to the letter, but wanted to clear this assignment up before she took some time off.

Josh's desk was still empty, and the assistant city editor didn't know when he'd return but suggested that she leave a message. A lot of good that'll do, she thought as she walked over to the darkroom. She had left Josh a message the previous afternoon also, but apparently he had chosen to ignore it.

"Well, that's fine with me," she said out loud. "If you're avoiding me and I'm avoiding you, we might just manage not to see so much of each other.''

''You say something, Tracy?'' Al asked.

She turned and saw her boss right behind her. She gave him an embarrassed smile. ''Just talking to myself,'' she explained. ''Say, is there any chance I can have next week off? My doctor's decided I work too hard.''

''Sure, we'll work something out,'' Al agreed. He picked up some folders from the top of the file and headed back toward the city room. ''Leave a note on my desk reminding me, will you?''

After doing that, Tracy kept herself occupied with odd jobs. She straightened up the darkroom and made a list of supplies that they were low on. She was cleaning out the darkroom sink when Bob came in.

''What an inspirational sight!'' he teased. ''You'll make someone a good little wife someday!''

She frowned at him. ''That type of remark will get something thrown at you,'' she said, pretending to be angry.

After Bob had spoken, he remembered her situation and was horrified. ''I didn't mean it,'' he hurried to apologize.

''I know,'' she assured him with a laugh. ''You may be a male chauvinist, but you're not cruel.''

Bob made a face. ''I have a feeling I've ruined my chances for getting you to do me a favor.''

Tracy rinsed out the sink, and then dried her hands. ''You never can tell. What do you want me to do?''

''I'm supposed to photograph that American Cancer Society dinner-dance this evening at the

Ritz-Carlton," he told her. "But it's my wife's birthday and she made reservations for us to go out to dinner. Could you cover for me?"

"Sure," Tracy shrugged. "Do I need to stay long?"

"No, just a couple of pictures will do it," he assured her.

The phone rang in the outer room and Bob went out to get it. After a minute or two, he called back in to Tracy. "I've got an accident to attend on the Kennedy Expressway. See you later."

When Tracy finished in the darkroom, the outer office was still deserted, but there was an envelope on the desk with her name typed on it. Wonderingly, she picked it up and opened it. A single piece of paper was inside. Spelled out, in letters cut from a newspaper, was the message:

CALL OFF THE INVESTIGATION OR ELSE

Tracy stared at it for a moment, not knowing whether to laugh or be frightened. This sort of melodrama was best left to the movies, she thought. Still, her next reaction was to pick up the phone and call Josh. He was in his office but not delighted to hear from her.

"What is it this time?" he snapped impatiently.

"It's about that story we were working on," she began. "There's a new development that I—"

"Look, I don't have time now," he cut in quickly. "I'm late for deadline. I'll get back to you."

Like you've returned all my other calls, she thought. "Don't bother." She was proud of her light and easy tone. "I'll send you a memo."

Maybe it wouldn't be so hard to work with Josh after all, she told herself as she hung up the phone. He still was an arrogant bastard and certainly not the least bit lovable.

Josh stared bleakly at the phone. It was true that he was late for deadline, but only because he couldn't concentrate on anything anymore. Everything he tried to do brought him memories of Tracy. He felt as if she were haunting him. It was no excuse to be so rude to her on the phone, he knew, but, God, it hurt so to hear her voice. He was fighting it the only way he knew how.

With determination, it took Josh another two hours to finish the article he had been writing. Then he leaned back in his chair with a sigh. What the hell was he going to do about Tracy?

"Mr. Rettinger?" He looked up to see one of the mailboys at his desk. "Here's your mail." He handed Josh an envelope and went back to his own desk.

In the envelope Josh found a note: "I got this today. Tracy." Very brief and to the point, he thought morosely, hurt that it was so businesslike. Well, what did he expect? he asked himself as he unfolded the enclosed paper.

His first reaction to the threatening letter was very much like Tracy's: he just stared at it for a long moment. Then he burst into rage. How dare someone send something like this to her! He jumped to his feet and was across the city room in a second.

"Where's Tracy?" he demanded of Al at the picture desk.

"On assignment," Al shrugged, then frowned when he saw Josh's face. "What's wrong?"

"Did she show you this?" Josh asked, handing him the letter.

Bob came over to look at it also. "That serious?" he asked with a half-laugh. "I wonder if he used the *Tribune*."

Josh turned a furious glance on him. "It's not funny!" he thundered. "Somebody who is stupid enough to do something like this is stupid enough to follow it through. She could be in danger!"

Al and Bob exchanged glances. "Now, hold on, Josh," Al said soothingly. "Let's think this through. The only investigation she's working on is that one with you, so it must be someone connected with that. Have you found anything out?"

"I found out that damn lawyer's in it up to his neck," Josh said savagely. "And I think it's time I insisted on seeing him." Grabbing the note from Al's hand, he flew toward the hallway.

"Whew!" Bob laughed slightly. "The man's on the rampage, and I thought I was going to be victim number one."

"Yeah, but ain't it kind of strange?" Al said thoughtfully. "For a cold fish who's never given a damn about anybody here, his behavior seems a little out of proportion."

"Hey, we've all become rather protective of Tracy since we found out she's pregnant," Bob pointed out. "Maybe old Rettinger has a heart, too."

Al gave him a strange look. "Or maybe he's got a guilty conscience."

Paul Hanson was deep in conference with Carl Philips, the newspaper's head lawyer. Finally, after doing scut work for months, he was getting into some real action. Maybe if he impressed Philips enough, he would be out of this backwater office.

"Well," he began. "I think we should—"

The door flew open and Josh burst in. "I've had it, Hanson," he cried. "You've gone too far."

Both lawyers had jumped to their feet at Josh's entrance and stared at him in astonishment. Miss D'Alessandro, Paul Hanson's secretary, came rushing in.

"I tried to stop him, Mr. Hanson," she explained. "Shall I call security?"

"Why not?" Josh growled, answering before the lawyer had a chance. "Maybe they'd like to hear why he's sending threatening notes to one of our photographers."

Mr. Philips frowned and looked at Hanson, whose face was red with anger as he fought to gain control of the situation. "I don't think we need to call security just yet," Hanson said hurriedly. "I'm certain this gentleman will be happy to wait in my outer office until I'm done here. Perhaps then I can learn what his problem is."

"I'm not going anywhere," Josh told him bluntly. "And you know damn well who I am. You've been doing your best to avoid me for the last two days."

Casting a worried glance at his superior, Hanson tried not to panic. "Oh, you must be Mr. Rettinger, one of our reporters," he said. "I'm sorry that I had to break our appointments, but I have been very busy. As you can see, I'm in conference now, and you wouldn't want to waste Mr. Philips's time."

Josh glanced at the other man. He was older, dressed expensively, and had an air of confidence about him. "Would it be such a waste of his time?" Josh asked. "He might like to hear about how you tried to get some incriminating photos into your hands by pretending to be representing the police. Unfortunately, you forgot to get one of the cops to back up your story."

"What's this all about, Hanson?" Mr. Philips asked sharply.

The younger man tried to laugh, but was too nervous to carry it off. "Just a little misunderstanding," he assured him. "I was doing a favor for a friend."

"I'll bet," Josh snapped. "The question is, how much is the friend paying you? Will it cover that debt of yours to the loan sharks, or will you just blow it on some woman?"

Miss D'Alessandro was listening with avid curiosity, while Mr. Philips's mood was one of growing anger. "What the devil is all this?"

"I'd be happy to explain," Josh said, turning to him. "A few days ago, Mr. Hanson here approached one of the paper's photographers and asked for the prints and negatives of some pictures she took at a police raid of a place suspected of homosexual prostitution. He said the pictures were for the police, but subsequent checking proved that he had lied. Further checking showed that he is deeply in debt. When I tried to talk to him, he repeatedly broke appointments."

"I happen to be a busy man, Rettinger," Hanson insisted haughtily. "I don't have time to talk to just anybody."

Josh gave Hanson a black look, and handed Mr. Philips the note. "The photographer got this today."

Mr. Philips looked at the note silently, then glanced up at Hanson. "Is this true?"

Hanson glared at Josh and at his secretary, then shrugged. "Well, I did talk with the fool woman." He jumped when Josh cursed angrily, only standing still because of a glance from Mr. Philips. "So I pretended that the police wanted the photos; what harm was there? A friend of mine had been innocently caught in the pictures and didn't want his career ruined because of it."

"So you lied?" Mr. Philips asked quietly. "Did that seem particularly ethical to you?"

"Hey, I wasn't hurting anybody," he insisted.

"What about this letter?" Josh demanded. "If nothing else, you as sure as hell were trying to scare her."

"Mr. Rettinger, please," Mr. Philips's voice was smooth and controlled, filled with authority. "I appreciate your bringing all this to my attention, and you may rest assured that I will handle it; but it may best be done in private. Let's keep this one out of the papers, okay?"

Josh stared at him for a moment before he realized he was being dismissed. "All right," he said slowly, with a hateful glance at Hanson. "But I want my chance at him."

"Believe me, he will probably prefer that I had left him to your mercy," Mr. Philips said, with a cold, calculating smile.

Josh could do little else but nod and leave the room. He felt rather disappointed, for he had wanted to grind Hanson's ass into the floor. He wasn't going to stand for people treating Tracy that way.

* * *

The Ritz-Carlton had been built to impress people, and it certainly did that. Its main lobby was on the twelfth floor, above apartments and the elite Water Tower Shopping Center. Down the hall from the lobby—complete with skylights and fountains—was the main ballroom, which had crystal prisms covering more than half the ceiling.

To reach the ballroom, one had to go through the lobby, down a long hallway past The Dining Room and the Terrace Bar, and past the private coat check and into a rather plain entry room. The plush carpet there, a deep rose color with diagonal stripes of gold, blended well with the pale marble trim around the floor's edge and the metallic gold-and-rose wallpaper. Lights recessed into the ceiling along the wall gave the room a muted glow.

Across this room and up a few steps one found oneself in a slightly more posh entry room. The carpet there was even softer to the touch, though paler in color. In the center was a floral pattern that was repeated in the floral arrangement that covered the gold antique table along the wall. A huge mirror hung behind it, and two antique chairs graced either side of it. Josh was not certain whether the chairs were actual antiques or just copies in the French provincial style, but he decided not to sit in them.

Across the room from the gold table were the doors to the ballroom, and the bar that adjoined it.

The ballroom itself was huge. A stage for a band or orchestra was along the far wall, and a good-sized dance floor in the middle. To either side of the stage, long red velvet drapes blocked off the windows.

Large floor-to-ceiling mirrors were placed regularly around the other walls. They reflected the well-dressed guests as they moved toward the round dinner tables. Silent waiters were just adding the finishing touches to the tables. Josh wondered what they would have to eat. He was starving and hoped that they'd eat soon.

"Josh, darling, you must come and meet Andrea," Denise whispered, tugging at his arm and pulling him away from the ballroom door. "You know, she practically organized this whole affair herself, so you must tell her what a wonderful time you're having."

Josh allowed her to direct him through the crowds of people standing about talking and laughing while they waited for the main ballroom to be opened for their dinner. He wasn't sure, though, just what Denise expected him to say to her wonderful Andrea Redmon. This type of one-hundred-dollar-a-plate formal dinner was not exactly his thing. He felt uncomfortable in the tuxedo he'd been forced to rent, and didn't have anything to say to all these people gathered around him. He was sorry he had let Denise talk him into escorting her.

They stopped walking and joined a group of people hovering about a tall, dark-haired woman in her late forties. One of the most recognized names in Chicago society, Andrea Redmon seemed to be a woman of boundless energy. Her interests and involvements ranged from the fine arts to running charity fund raisers, such as this dinner-dance for the American Cancer Society. As much as he might admire the good she did, Josh had little interest in actually meeting her and was wondering how late Denise would want to stay, when three of the people moved away and Denise pulled him up to Andrea.

"Why, Denise, I had no idea you were going to attend," Andrea said after the introductions were made. "Is this one of your pet charities?"

Denise's smile could have melted the polar ice cap. "Why, yes," she confided. "And I wanted to be sure to attend since you were running it."

Josh silently gave Denise a few points for astuteness. Maybe she ought to give up acting and go into politics.

"Why, how sweet of you," Andrea sighed. "I just wish you could sit at our table, but it's filled already. Chairmen of the board, some local politicians; you understand."

Josh did, and silently wondered how Denise would try to dispose of one of them. He turned slightly to watch the crowd as Denise and Andrea continued to talk, starting suddenly when his eyes lit on a man in his mid-thirties with a white streak in the front of his dark hair.

"Do you know who that man is?" he asked Andrea, unaware that he was interrupting an eloquent plea of Denise's that was supposed to get them seats at Andrea's table.

Unmoved by Denise's eloquence, Andrea was quick to seize on Josh's interruption and look where he was indicating. "Oh, that's William Langdon," she said. "He's with the American National Bank; they loaned him to us to help with the financial side of the dance. Do you know him?"

"I might," Josh said noncommittally, and glanced back at Denise. "If you ladies will excuse me, I think I'll go have a word with him."

Before Denise could indicate her displeasure,

he left. By some stroke of luck, Langdon moved away from the couple he was speaking to just as Josh approached him.

"Mr. Langdon?" he stopped in the man's way. "I'm Josh Rettinger from the *Tribune.*"

William Langdon looked neither worried nor impressed, but Josh went on. "I don't believe that we've actually met before, but I recognized your face." That brought a slight wariness into Langdon's eyes and he glanced about him, as if fearing they might be overheard.

"You may even remember the picture," Josh continued. "It was taken about a week ago at an electronic-games parlor."

"I'm afraid you have made a mistake," the other man insisted rather coldly. "I don't have the slightest idea what you're talking about." He started to move away, but Josh followed him.

"It was pretty funny, really," Josh said chattily, as if they were having a normal conversation. "Those pictures were filed away and forgotten until one of our lawyers tried to get hold of them. Suddenly everybody got real interested in who was in them."

Langdon's face paled, and he turned to face Josh. "Look, Rettinger, whatever your scheme is, it's not going to work. I'm not stupid enough to agree to blackmail." He kept his voice low, but it cracked with fear.

Josh's smile was far from pleasant. "Judge everyone by your own standards, eh, Langdon?" he said quietly. "Well, I'm not interested in blackmail. I much prefer a good story, though I'll admit as it stands now there isn't one. But when bribery, harassment, and physical threats are added, it begins to attract more interest.''

A couple came over to greet the banker and he was forced to smile politely. Once they moved away, he grabbed Josh's arm and nodded toward a door in the wall behind them. Josh followed him into the ballroom, where waiters were placing baskets of dinner rolls on the tables. They moved over to the near wall.

"Now look here," Langdon said. "I'll admit that I tried to get those pictures, but I didn't bribe or harass or threaten anybody. I just paid Hanson to do a job for me. I'm not responsible for his stupidity.''

"I think that point could be argued," Josh told him coldly. "But I don't intend to bother. I just want to make the newspaper's position clear. Your sexual preferences are your own business. They become our business when you make them into a story for us.''

Langdon nodded. "I understand," he said, his manner as subdued as his voice. "I'll tell Hanson to back off.''

"I think he already has." Josh's laugh was short; then he turned and left the ballroom.

Denise was waiting for him, and took his arm again as soon as she saw him. From the look on her face, he suspected that she had not succeeded in getting a spot at Andrea's table. He wondered if she was disappointed enough to want to leave, so he could go over to Tracy's and tell her about Langdon.

As if his thoughts could work magic, he suddenly saw Tracy across the room. Her camera around her neck, she was jotting down something in a small notebook, probably names to go with the pictures she had taken. She was wearing a dark green dress belted lightly around the loose-fitting waist. It was a simple and much less dressy style than Denise's long black affair, but to Josh she looked gorgeous. He couldn't turn away.

Perhaps Tracy sensed him watching her, for she looked up abruptly and her eyes met his. For a split second, her face radiated love, then it went cold and expressionless as Denise moved over closer to him, muttering something that he paid no attention to. Instinctively, he took a step toward Tracy, but as Denise's presence stopped him, Tracy turned away and was lost to his sight.

"Where are you going?" Denise snapped, well aware of his lack of attention. "They've opened the ballroom and we're supposed to find our seats."

He glanced at her in irritation, then back to the spot where Tracy had disappeared. With a sigh, he turned and went with Denise into the ballroom. Once he dumped her at the table, he promised himself, he would come back and find Tracy.

Lord, was there no way to avoid him? Tracy thought angrily. She had thought this evening would turn out to be fairly pleasant, but, no, he had to be here to spoil things.

For the first time in weeks, she had had a decent dinner. It was only scrambled eggs and toast, but she'd kept it down and felt almost human afterward. She had dressed carefully for her assignment, trying not to appear as part of the paying crowd, but not conspicuously different either. After she finished the assignment, she was even considering taking in a movie at the Water Tower Theatre downstairs. Now all she wanted to do was go home and cry.

Taking a deep breath, she forced herself to continue her picture taking. Thank God, she only had a few left. One with the mayor and Ms. Redmon, and another of the Cancer Society's board of directors. Maybe she could get them done without having to see that hateful blonde hanging all over Josh.

Tracy finished the end of the roll in the ballroom, snapping the pictures at the various tables. Then she hurried across the now-deserted entry rooms to get her coat and camera case from the checkroom. She put everything down on a sofa in the hallway outside the checkroom to pack her equipment.

"Hello, Tracy."

She spun around to find Josh standing behind her. Denise was nowhere in sight.

"Hello, Josh," she said. The lightness of her voice contrasted with the heaviness of her heart. "I didn't know you came to these charity affairs." To avoid looking at him, she went back to packing her case.

"I got roped into it," he admitted reluctantly.

"Well, you'll have a good time, and the food is always great," she told him bracingly. After zipping up her case, she put it over her shoulder, picked up her coat and walked past him. Although the effort almost killed her, she did not look back at him, pretending instead to be interested in the elaborate waterfall that fell over rocks in front of the Terrace Bar. The sound of the water was refreshing, as was the piano playing on a little island near the waterfall.

"I think that whole mess with Hanson is over."

His voice was right behind her and she silently damned the waterfall, music, and thick carpeting that had muffled his footsteps.

"That's good," she said. He was too close to her and she felt afraid. Why was he trying to hurt her again?

The corridor back to the lobby suddenly seemed a mile long, and she felt as if she had to reach it quickly or she'd be lost again in Josh's smile. She quickened her steps on the beige, blue, and green carpeting, and tried to still the panic that rose as she realized he was still with her.

"I met the guy who wanted the pictures," he went on. "The rising young executive type."

Tracy barely heard him, for she was desperate to get away. She had passed two sitting areas, but still had more to go. The hallway seemed to be getting longer rather than shorter. The mirrored panels that covered part of the walls were set at angles and she seemed to be floating in them, but never getting any closer. Each step became an effort as her fear of Josh's presence grew. She felt warm and suddenly short of breath and the walls seemed to dance around her.

Oh, God, make him go away, she silently prayed. Make him go away so I can breathe again.

"Hey, you'd better sit down," Josh was saying somewhere from a distance and she felt him lead her over to a sofa.

Her legs felt less wobbly once she was seated and a miraculous breeze seemed to float out of The Dining Room. She leaned back, letting her coat slide down to the seat next to her, and took a deep breath.

"Let me get you some water," Josh said. He sounded concerned and his eyes were worried.

"No." Her voice was amazingly strong, and it stopped him as he turned toward the nearby restaurant. "No, I'm fine. You can go back to your party."

"Don't be silly," he said with a frown. "You need some help. Let me get you a drink and then I'll take you home."

"No," she repeated, her voice a little louder. She looked at him coldly, no trace of warmth on her face. "I don't want a drink of water from you or a ride home. I don't want anything from you."

Josh was not a patient man. "You obviously aren't well," he snapped. "And I'm going to—"

"You're going to leave me alone," she cried angrily. "Can't you understand? I don't want anything from you! Nothing! I don't want to see you. I don't want to talk to you. And I don't want your help." She rose to her feet, and was relieved to find that her dizziness had passed. "I am fine, but even if I weren't, I'd rather pass out on the floor and be stepped on than accept your help."

Josh's face had gotten deathly white as she spoke, but she did not care. Neither did she care that her anger had attracted an interested group of spectators. She was finally fighting back and felt much stronger. For her baby's sake, she was going to win.

"Tracy . . ." he pleaded quietly.

She turned and picked up her coat from the brown leather sofa, then faced him. Her head was high and her voice was clear. "Go to hell, Josh." She turned and left him standing there.

Chapter Thirteen

TRACY BURIED HER HEAD deeper under her pillow, but it didn't help block out the sound. Daisy, her newest stray, was far under her bed and barking her head off.

"Oh, shut up, Daisy," Tracy muttered sleepily. "You're not big enough to scare anything away."

A bit of light had somehow filtered under her blanket and pillow, so Tracy turned over before letting herself fall back asleep. After being awake all night, feeling miserable and depressed, it was so wonderful to find some relief in sleep. She had no idea what time it was and did not care. Daisy didn't eat until afternoon, and Milton, the old blind Persian cat that had replaced Cookie and her kittens, had plenty of dry food that he could get to easily. There was nothing to do but relax.

A weight on one side of the bed roused her slightly, but only enough to shift her body comfortably before she drifted away again. Even the pulling aside of part of her blanket registered only faintly on her mind.

"Tracy?" A hand brushed back the curls from her face, moving with such gentleness and love that it had to be part of a dream. "Tracy?"

She sighed and rolled over on her back, her eyes opening slowly to find Josh sitting on the edge of her bed. She frowned at him. "What are you doing here? How'd you get in?"

"I still have a key," he admitted. "And I came because I was worried about you. You were sick last night, and I was afraid that you hadn't made it home safely."

She rolled over on her stomach, her face turned away from him. "Well, I did," she said amid a yawn. "Now go away and let me sleep."

The weight disappeared and so apparently did Josh, for he said nothing else. Tracy dozed briefly until his presence actually registered on her mind. Then she sat up with a start, and glared at him when she found him sitting in the chair next to the bed. "What do you want?" she demanded.

"I told you," he began.

"No, you didn't. There is such a thing as a telephone, you know. If you were so worried, why didn't you just call?"

"I've been calling all day," he snapped. "And got no answer."

Tracy glanced at her clock. It was past two in the afternoon. "I didn't hear the phone," she admitted slowly. She shook her head, trying to rid herself of that thick feeling of confusion that surrounded her. "It was late by the time I got to sleep."

"It was for me, too," he said with a nod of agreement.

Tracy's eyes were narrow with suspicion as she glanced coldly at him. She had her own interpretation of that. "Yes, I saw Denise all over you last night."

Tracy's continuous presumptions used up his small supply of patience. He jumped to his feet angrily. "Tracy, stop it!" he cried. "Why do you keep trying to punish me? I feel awful enough about all of this."

She lay back on her pillows with a hollow laugh. "Tell me about how bad you feel!" she said bitterly. "Tell me how you can't eat and when you do, it won't stay in your stomach. Tell me how you feel weak and dizzy and want only to cry!"

"Tracy . . ." Josh's anger was gone as fast as it had come, and his voice was pleading.

"No, don't tell me anything," she said abruptly and turned on her side so she could not see him. "Just go home and leave me alone. Maybe if you're lucky, I'll lose the baby and you won't have to feel guilty about anything."

Josh was over to the bed in an instant. "How the hell can you say that?" he cried, taking hold of her shoulder and pulling her over to face him. "I don't want you to lose the baby!"

"No?" she asked. Sudden tears ran down her face, blurring the image of the angry face that hovered above her. "Wouldn't that make things much simpler for you? Who knows, maybe I'd even be stupid enough to start up with you again! But with birth control pills this time!"

"Tracy, stop it!" he shouted. His hands on her shoulders, he shook her. "Stop it!"

The tears came faster now, and she gazed up at him. Her anger was gone, leaving the full devastation of her heart in her eyes for him to see. "Why are you here?" she whispered in desperation. "Why can't you just leave me alone?"

Josh's anger had fled also and so had his desire to fight the feelings that he knew were so right. Gathering her up into his arms, he tried to soothe away the sobs that racked her body. "I can't stay away. I love you," he said, with the wonder of discovery. "I love you."

"But . . ." She pulled away from him slightly to stare up into his face.

Josh laid her back against the pillows, gently and with exquisite care. He kissed her forehead, then her eyes, and finally her mouth, with soft, almost reverent kisses. "I don't know what happened. I don't care anymore. I just know that I can't live like this. I love you too much to be apart from you again."

She just stared up at him, her eyes almost afraid to hope.

"Now, what's this about losing the baby?" he asked her gently. "Was it just a wild threat to hurt me, or did your doctor actually warn you?"

She shook her head slowly. "He said I'm not getting enough rest or food, and I have to take at least a week off from work." Her eyes never left his face. Was this all some wild dream?

"Well, that's easily fixed," he told her briskly and got to his feet. He found the suitcase in Tracy's closet and opened it on the end of the bed; then he took handfuls of clothes from her drawers and dumped them in.

Stunned, she watched him for a few seconds before she found her voice. "What are you doing?"

"I'm taking you up to my parents' house," he said simply, not bothering to stop while he spoke. He tossed in a comb and brush he found on her dresser and then disappeared into the bathroom. "How much of this junk do you need?" he called to her.

224

She got to her feet and stumbled to the bathroom. "Let me do that," she insisted, but somehow she was swept up in his arms and carried back to bed.

"You don't need any of it because you're going to spend the next week in bed," he informed her, then stomped back off to the bathroom.

Tracy sat up on her bed and pulled a few pieces of clothing from the mess in her suitcase.

"What are you doing?" Josh snapped when he came back from the bathroom with her shampoo and toothbrush.

"Getting dressed," she pointed out. "I don't usually go visiting in my nightgown."

He shrugged his shoulders. "Okay, if you want to," he grudgingly allowed. "But you aren't going visiting, you're going to get some rest. It seems sort of dumb to change now and then change back as soon as you get there." He went over to her closet and stared inside. "Where's the cat carrier?"

In less than a half hour, she was installed in the back of his car, wrapped in her blanket, and ordered to go to sleep. Milton was in a cat carrier on the front seat next to Josh, and Daisy was relegated to the back after biting him when he tried to get her out from under the bed.

For a while, Tracy stared at the back of Josh's head, unable to believe that he had come back into her life, unable to believe that he loved her; but the soothing motion of the car was too much to resist, and she let it lull her to sleep. When she awoke, the car was stopped and Josh was nudging her gently.

"Wake up, sleepyhead," he teased.

She opened her eyes slowly, afraid that all the rest had just been a dream, but he was there, smiling at her, his eyes filled with love. Tenderly, he helped her from the car and then picked her up in his arms.

"Hey, I can walk," she protested.

"For the last month, we've both been through hell. Let me pamper you a little," he pleaded softly.

The air seemed remarkably warm on her face as he carried her from the car up to the house. It was as if the winter had disappeared with her sorrows.

Josh's mother opened the door before he had a chance to knock. She stared at them in astonishment.

"Josh, is something wrong?" Her face reflected concern.

Josh shook his head as he carried Tracy into the living room. His father was there and so was Monica.

"Nothing at all," he insisted proudly. "We're having a baby, and Tracy needed some rest."

Tracy buried her head against Josh's neck, for his words had such special meaning for her. He had accepted the baby! He really did love her!

With her face hidden as it was, Tracy did not see the defiant glare on Josh's face as he dared anyone to dispute his words. Neither did she see the look of surprise that his parents exchanged.

"Josh, that's wonderful," his mother exclaimed after a stunned moment. "We'd love to have her rest up here."

"It's where she belongs," his father agreed.

Satisfied, Josh let Tracy get to her feet. "I'll get her stuff from the car."

"This is very exciting," Mrs. Rettinger told Tracy.

She smiled, aware that Monica was watching her strangely, and folded up the blanket that Josh had carried in with her. "I really feel rather embarrassed that he brought me up here this way," she admitted.

"Nonsense," the older woman shook her head. "Now, tell me before I burst: When is the baby due?"

"She's not telling anyone anything right now," Josh said suddenly, appearing in the doorway with the cat carrier and Daisy. "If she sleeps for the few hours before dinner, I may let her get up for a while. She can answer all your questions then."

"Josh!" his mother protested his high-handedness with a laugh. "You mustn't order her around so."

He looked at Tracy. Her eyes glowed with love; it was clear that she did not share his mother's protests. "I'm only following her doctor's orders," he explained and nodded toward the stairs. "You know where my room is? Upstairs with you, then."

Tracy smiled at his parents. "I'm afraid he's right," she admitted.

"Then get going," Mr. Rettinger said. Paddy had already been making Daisy's acquaintance, and he joined him. "Just us tell us their names."

"Daisy's the dog, and Milton's the cat," Tracy called as she went toward the stairs. "Neither's a diabetic, but Milton's blind."

As she went the rest of the way up the stairs, she heard Mr. Rettinger talking soothingly to the animals. It was good to be back here and not have to feel weighed down by everything. With all the strains of the past few weeks removed, she had to admit she was exhausted.

She went into Josh's room. The drapes were open, letting in warmth and sunshine to welcome her. Walking over to the windows, she looked down on the front of the house. Along the sidewalk were splotches of color: blue and yellow and white.

Hearing a sound behind her, Tracy turned to see Monica come in. She was carrying a pile of clean sheets. "Aunt Clara asked me to make up the bed for you," she explained.

Tracy nodded and looked back out the window. "Are those flowers along the walk?" she asked.

"There are some crocuses down there," Monica said offhandedly as she unfolded the first sheet. "They usually bloom in early spring."

Gazing out the window, Tracy realized that spring had come to her heart also, for she suddenly felt lighthearted and happy.

"I imagine that Josh was rather surprised that he was about to become a father," Monica said quietly.

Tracy found something in Monica's voice that she did not entirely like, and turned around to face her. "We were both quite happy about it," she said.

Monica just smiled innocently as she tucked the sheet under the mattress. "Of course you were. It's just that I know that Josh never wanted any kids, and I thought—"

"What makes you so certain he didn't want children?" Tracy asked her quickly. "Just because you two never had any . . ." She let her voice drift away meaningfully.

"Oh, let's cut out the crap," Monica said, straightening up. "We both know that I told Josh that he was sterile. What I want to know is, what is he going to do about it?" Her eyes were hard and calculating, but Tracy thought she saw a flicker of worry in them.

"You told him?" Tracy was puzzled and leaned against the windowsill. "But I thought he said he went to a doctor."

Monica sighed impatiently. "He did, but I made the appointment for the day before he went out of town. Since he wouldn't be around, he told the doctor to tell me the results." She shrugged indifferently. "It was really too easy. A little lie and a few tears and I had the divorce that I wanted."

"But that's terrible!" Tracy jumped to her feet, shocked. "All these years, you've let him believe your lie!"

Monica unfolded the top sheet and snapped it crisply in the air. "It's hardly the criminal offense you seem to think," she scoffed. "Josh didn't want kids. He didn't really want a wife, either. Just someone to cook and keep the house reasonably clean. Anyone would do to keep his bed warm." She straightened the sheet and then looked up at Tracy. "So now that he knows, what's he going to do?"

"What do you expect him to do?" Tracy demanded, a frown of annoyance creasing her forehead. She certainly did not like this woman! "Take out an ad in the paper?"

Monica bit her lip impatiently. "I have a position here in the community. You can mock it all you like, but I've worked hard for the place I have and I don't want it jeopardized. It was hard

229

enough coming back here after the divorce and being accepted. If it gets out that I lied to get it, I might as well move!''

"What is this? Confession time?'' Josh asked from the doorway.

Monica spun around, her face white at first; but slowly her natural color returned.

Josh brought Tracy's suitcase into the room and put it down next to the dresser. Tracy was certain from the mild look on his face that he had no idea what she and Monica had been discussing. Would Monica bring it up or should she?

"Oh, don't play dumb!" Monica jeered. "I have a right to know. Just how much are you going to tell people? What are you going to tell Aunt Clara and Uncle John?''

Josh's confused glance went from his ex-wife to Tracy. As much as she hoped to avoid this admission in front of Monica, Tracy knew she'd have to explain things. "Monica lied about the doctor's report. She's afraid that if it gets out, it'll ruin her social position.''

Josh turned to stare at Monica in disbelief. "You lied about my being sterile?'' he whispered harshly. "For all these years, you've let me think I was?''

Monica stared back at him, then started to laugh slowly. "My God, you didn't know! I should have kept my mouth shut! You didn't know!''

Josh ignored her words, if he even heard them. "Damnit, Monica! Did you hate me that much?'' His voice was an agony that hurt Tracy to hear.

"Oh, no, you don't," Monica cried. "You aren't going to put all the blame on me. You forced me into it! That was the only way that I could have gotten my divorce!''

"What the hell are you talking about?" he cried angrily. "You never asked for one. What makes you think I wanted to hold on to that farce of a relationship?"

"Well, you certainly seemed to," Monica insisted, apprehensive now of his growing rage.

"Our marriage was nothing. Nothing!" he cried. "We had no relationship at all. What was there to keep?"

"That doesn't answer my question," she pointed out. Her face had paled slightly, although her tone was almost as belligerent. "What are you going to tell your parents?"

"How about the truth?" Josh snapped.

Tracy went over to step in front of him, her right hand gently on his chest, while she turned to watch Monica. "We don't want to build our happiness on the unhappiness of another," she said slowly. "What you did was terrible, but it's over." She felt Josh protest slightly and pressed harder. "Let us talk about it by ourselves. If we decide to tell Josh's parents the truth, we will warn you first."

Monica nodded reluctantly, then, after a quick glance at Josh's unforgiving face, she hurried from the room. "I really only wanted my freedom," she said at the door. Josh made another sudden move and she darted out. Tracy sighed and leaned into Josh's arms.

"What is there to talk about?" Josh asked her. "She's a bitch and deserves to be exposed as one."

"Why?" Tracy asked quietly. "Will it undo the pain that she caused? You heard her. All that she's worried about is her social position. Not her family, not Charlie, just her social position. Don't you feel sorry for someone who has so little?''

He moved away from her and went over to the window. ''She's got what is important to her,'' he pointed out stubbornly. ''What she bought for herself with her lie. Is it fair that she should go on as if nothing had happened? Be welcomed here as if she were the wronged ex-wife?''

''Oh, Josh,'' Tracy sighed. ''Was she ever really welcomed here? From what your father said at Christmas, they only tolerate her because of Charlie.''

He turned to face her. ''That doesn't make it any easier to see her here every time I come home. See her pretending to care about Mom and Dad.''

''So tell them the truth if you want,'' she said. ''I would imagine they'd figure it out by themselves anyway. I just don't think we need to destroy Monica to be happy. Our happiness is inside us. I rose above David and you can rise above Monica.''

She could see the pain in his eyes and ached to help him. She walked over, stopping just before him. ''It doesn't matter anymore,'' she told him softly. ''It's over.''

He looked down into her face, his eyes confused and hurt. ''How can you say that after what I almost did to you? To us?''

He walked past her to the edge of his bed and sank down, staring at his hands. ''God, I've been such a fool,'' he cried. ''She's the one who gave me the doctor's report, and I never doubted her word. Even when you kept insisting that it was our child, it never occurred to me that Monica might

have lied. I always thought *you* had to be lying."
He turned to look up at her. "How can you ever
forgive me?"

"Oh, Josh," she sighed, coming over to the bed
also. She remained standing, cradling his head
against her chest. His arms lightly embraced her.
"It wasn't your fault. You weren't deliberately trying to hurt me."

"But what if I hadn't come to my senses and realized that I loved you?" he asked her. "I would
never have learned the truth and you would have
had the baby all alone."

"You don't know me very well, if you think I'd
give up that easily," she laughed, her fingers running through his hair and over his shoulders. It felt
so good to touch him again. "I am certain that the
baby is going to look just like you, complete with
your forbidding scowl. I had great plans to take
him to see you, and then you would have been
forced to admit you were the father."

"How can you be so generous?"

"It's easy because I'm so happy," she whispered. He pulled his head away from her slightly
as she looked down at him. Then she bent down,
her mouth touching his. Their kiss was sweet and
filled with promises, and it seemed to ease the agony from Josh's soul.

"Oh, Tracy," he sighed. "Do you know what
you do to me?"

She smiled down at him, confident in his love.

"You make the most unreasonable things seem
right." His hands moved over her in a light caress.
"I won't say anything," he agreed. "For our sake,
not Monica's. I don't know that I'll be able to look

her in the face again—but I'd rather watch you any-way."

Tracy smiled and kissed him gently. "If she's got any sense, she'll make herself invisible while we're here visiting, especially after the baby's born."

"Speaking of Josh Junior," Josh said suddenly, with a stern look at her. "You are supposed to be resting, aren't you?"

Tracy got a gleam in her eye as she glanced at him and then the bed. "Actually, I'm not all that tired," she pointed out.

He moved her away from him as he rose to his feet. "Oh, no, you don't," he scolded her lightly. "When we get back to Chicago, we're going to see your doctor to find out what we can and cannot do. Until then, the only thing you're going to do in bed is sleep."

"Yes, sir," she sighed. "But I'll miss you."

Josh had begun to finish making the bed and turned to frown at her. "Hey, I'm not going any-where. You're stuck with me forever." His smile was warm as he pulled her into his arms for a soft and loving kiss.

Tracy relaxed in his arms. Their spring had come at last.

THE CAVE DREAMERS

JEANNE WILLIAMS

THE CAVE DREAMERS is a vivid, passionate novel of the lives and loves of the women across centuries who share the secret of "The Cave of Always Summer." From the dawn of time to the present, the treasured mystery of the cave is passed and guarded, joining generation to generation through their dreams and desires.
83501-0/$7.95

An **AVON** Trade Paperback

THE AVON ROMANCE

RANSOMED HEART April 1983
SPARKY ASCANI

A lovely young woman offers to sell her jewelry to pay her father's gambling debts but the buyer, a dashing jewelry designer, will accept nothing less than the most precious jewel of all—Analisa! The twosome must overcome separation and danger before Analisa's ransomed heart is free to love. 83287-9/$2.95

NOW COMES THE SPRING May 1983
ANDREA EDWARDS

Adventurous, creative newspaper photographer Tracy Monroe agrees to pose as the fiancee of cool, tough-talking star reporter Josh Rettinger because he can't face Christmas with his family alone. But their role playing becomes more than make believe, offering them unexpected feelings of desire...and a passion that brings the warmth of spring. 83329-8/$2.95

AVON Paperbacks

Available wherever paperbacks are sold or directly from the publisher. Include 50¢ per copy for postage and handling: allow 6-8 weeks for delivery. Avon Books, Mail Order Dept., 224 W. 57th St., N.Y., N.Y. 10019

Avon Romance 4-8